Siren's Lure

Copyright

Cover by Daqri Bernado
Formatting by Jaye Cox
Editing by First Reads Edits
Proofreading by Holmes Edits

The Kingdoms

Table of Contents

Siren's Lure

Nothing is as it seems.

Hayjen never believed in myths and nightmares until
he came face to face with one. Captured and trapped
on a slaver ship, life looks utterly grim. But when
mutiny and danger arise, Hayjen is tossed into the
ocean's watery depths where death stalks.

Vengeance is Lilja's middle name. As pirate captain
of the Sirenidae, she's made it her life goal to destroy
Scythia after what they've stolen from her. After one
miscalculation, she finds herself cast into the sea with
a man's life in her hands. Despite her laws ringing in
her mind, she saves him, exposing a secret she's kept
for years.

A secret that could destroy an entire race.

Chapter One

Hayjen

Life was never simple. Months on the cursed ship taught him that.

Hayjen stared from his floating prison at the death trap surrounding him. The seductive black waves lapped below, beckoning, whispering to him to take the chance, to seize his freedom. Luminescent coral cast soft light below the obsidian waves offering a lie, a hope that one could survive the harsh sea if one stayed in the light, but Hayjen knew better. Just past the comforting glow of the coral, a beast hunted—so deadly that no one chanced the sea at night.

He shivered as a shiny, midnight fin sliced through the water, before silently disappearing into the inky waves.

A Leviathan.

He wouldn't make it two arms' lengths before it dragged him below and killed him. His lips lifted into a grim smile. It might not be such a bad way to go compared to what the Scythians had planned for him.

"Hayjen?" a small voice called.

Turning his head, he sought out the unruly mop of white blond hair. Mer, a little girl who had been captured a couple weeks after he had, peeked at him over the top of a barrel. Her soft lilac eyes crinkled at the corners as she smiled at him, revealing a large gap where her tooth used to be. She scuttled from behind the barrel and slipped her small hand into his, their cuffs clinking together.

"What are you doing?"

What was he doing?

Hayjen stared at the tiny pale hand in his rough tan one. He could see her blue veins through her delicate skin. Mer was so fragile. His heart squeezed. This was why he couldn't escape. His gaze latched on to her sweet face, gazing at him with adoration. He couldn't leave Mer to the Scythians' cruelty. For some reason, they delighted in tormenting the little one. If he hadn't stepped in and given her some of his slop, she would've starved a long time ago. He also had his sister to think of. Where was she now? Was she okay?

"Hayjen?"

Hayjen blew out a breath and gave Mer his most brilliant smile. "I'm enjoying the view."

Her lilac eyes darted to the rolling black waves—they widened with excitement when a fin cut through the water. Mer stabbed a finger at the water, practically bouncing on her toes. "A Leviathan!"

"Only you would get excited over a Leviathan."

"They're nice. When I get bigger, I want one as a pet."

That made him snort. "I doubt that they would want to be kept as a pet." He tickled her neck. "I think they would probably want to snack on you."

Mer giggled. "No, they just like the way I smell. One sniffed me today."

Hayjen stiffened. What was she talking about? He knelt and placed his hands on her dainty shoulders. "How did they sniff you?" he questioned, attempting to keep his heart from beating out of his chest.

A little shrug. "I was hot, so I asked if I could go for a swim, and the mean man threw me in. The Leviathan were happy to have someone to play with."

Bile burned the back of his throat. They had thrown a little girl into Leviathan-infested waters? Unconsciously, his hands started to skim over her for injuries. "You swam with the Leviathan?" he croaked, trying to not throw up as he said the words.

Her innocent smile almost broke his heart. "Yep! We played tag. They darted in and bumped me with their noses before speeding off. I wish I was that fast in the water. When I got tired, one let me hold onto its fin. I got to ride one, Hayjen! Mama always said that one day I would be able to."

He sucked in a deep breath and considered Mer's unique lilac eyes. "You must not swim with the Leviathan again, Mer. It's dangerous."

"But they're my friends."

"I understand you had a wonderful time today, but they're not safe."

"They didn't hurt me."

"No more, Mer."

Her jaw jutted out stubbornly. "I like them."

If reason wasn't going to work, he had to scare her. "They like to eat people."

Her eyes bulged. "Eat people?" she squeaked.

"Yes." He nodded gravely. "Leviathan eat people, and I love you too much for you to be eaten, so please stay out of the water, for me." Hayjen watched her emotions flicker across her face until settling into resignation.

"I guess. I don't want to be eaten."

"Me neither." He pulled her into his arms and

hugged her tightly. She could have died. Those bastards threw her in the water expecting her to be eaten. Fury boiled through his veins. She was just a little girl. Dropping a kiss onto the crown of her head, Hayjen pulled back and chucked her under the chin. "It's time for bed, little one."

"Awww..." she pouted.

"None of that. Let's go."

Mer skipped ahead, and bounded down the stairs leaving him behind. He took one last look at the sea, and put his fantasies of freedom behind him. There wouldn't be any escape for him tonight. Hayjen strode to the stairs and descended into the belly of the ship. He wove around hammocks swaying from the ceiling, filled with sleeping slaves. He was one of the few men captured. Hayjen hadn't believed the rumors that Scythians were stealing people. He was minding his own business fishing one day when he was stolen. His rigging was tied up, the ship approached and offered him help. They looked like a run of the mill merchant ship right up until the moment they knocked him out. When he woke up, he was cuffed to the wall bleeding with no idea where he was. He was alone at first, that is until Mer was captured a few weeks later. She looked so pitiful, sopping wet and shaking like a leaf. When she wouldn't stop crying, one of the men cuffed her so hard behind the ear, she flew forward into the mast unconscious. Hayjen made a decision then. He'd protect her.

She was a peculiar little girl, but she had wormed her way into his heart immediately. Even now, months later, he still didn't know much about her family. Mer couldn't remember much. He didn't know if it was due to the blow to her head, her age, or her mind protecting her from a traumatic event.

Hayjen spotted Mer swinging in her hammock. Carefully, he caught it, and gave her a stern look. "It's time for bed."

"Okay." She snuggled down and looked up at him expectantly. "A song?"

Her angelic face, so full of hope, ensnared him. How could he say no? "One song. Just one." He knelt down next to her and sang a song his mum used to sing to him as a child. Her eyes hooded as sleep tried to take her. At the end, she slipped her hand into his.

"Prayer?"

"Anything for you, baby girl." He didn't feel particularly thankful at the moment, but it calmed her. After uttering a few words of thanks, her little eyes closed and stayed closed. Hayjen brushed the blond fuzz from her cheek, admiring the planes of her face. She reminded him of his sister Gwen. After their parents died, he would tuck her into bed and say a prayer with her, even though he was only a handful of years older than she was.

Mer released a soft sigh and smiled in her sleep. He could have lost her today. Rage bubbled at the thought. They had thrown her into Leviathan-infested waters. How did she survive? Leviathan were known for being extremely aggressive and eating just about anything. It didn't make sense. He dropped a kiss on her forehead and wove through the swinging hammocks. He needed to have a word with the captain. He most likely would receive a whipping for saying anything. It wasn't the first time, nor would it be the last.

When Hayjen spotted Leth, it was all he could do not to tear his head off. Leth was an extremely tall, widely-built man with cheekbones so sharp you could cut yourself on them. The first mate had a particularly mean streak. He enjoyed causing suffering and pain. Hayjen had received lashes for just looking at the man the wrong way. He blew out a breath—he needed to execute this with care. Steeling himself, he strode toward Leth. The Scythian first mate spotted him and jerked his chin towards Hayjen, pulling the other Scythians' attention. He clenched his jaw at the slurs thrown his way and halted before the group. "I need to speak with the captain."

Leth pushed off his chair and moved to stand in front of him. "The slave demands to see the captain. What does a slave need with the captain?"

Hayjen tipped his chin up to meet the first mate's eyes. "One of his slaves almost died today."

Leth chuckled, his cronies joining in. "Why would the captain care about that?"

"Mer was thrown into the sea."

Leth's face screwed up in disgust. "She was unscathed the last time I saw the little brat, unfortunately."

Several men crossed themselves. Something about Mer unnerved them and stirred their hate something fierce. "You threw her to the Leviathan."

"What concern is it of yours? She's not your daughter."

He wasn't getting anywhere arguing with this lout. "I think our captain would be very concerned that his first mate threw one of his valuables overboard."

The laughter cut off and Leth's eyes narrowed, taking on a menacing glint. "Are you threatening me, slave?" His tone took on a dangerous edge.

"No," Hayjen replied softly. "I am giving you my oath that if the little girl is harmed, I will make the

Leviathan look tame."

Waves crashed against the ship as the air around them filled with tension. "You dare to speak to me this way?" hissed Leth. "You are nothing but a blight on this world. Tonight you will be taught a lesson you will never forget, boy."

"So be it. It will change nothing."

The first mate seemed to swell in size, towering over Hayjen. "Tie him to the mast."

He didn't fight as he was roughly seized and dragged to the mast. It didn't matter if he fought. In the beginning, he had fought, but quickly he had learned they were all unnaturally stronger than him. Every once in a while, he would land a blow, but the majority of the time it was he that was hurt. Chain clipped into his metal manacle and bit into the abused flesh around his wrists. His hands were lifted above his head and his shirt cut from his back, exposing his healing lash marks to the cool air. This was going to hurt. He had calmed down for the sake of the girls on the ship to protect them as much as he could. One of the girls, Lera, had refused to sleep with a Scythian and was sentenced to forty lashes for disgracing her betters. He had stepped in and taken the punishment for her. She wouldn't have survived the lashing.

"Slave," Leth's voice leered. "Your very existence

sickens me."

A sharp whistle, and then blinding pain. Hayjen choked back a cry as tears stung his eyes. It never got easier. He never became immune to the pain.

"You think you're better than us, but you're not."

More pain.

"You're worthless."

His flesh opened.

"When the time comes, taking your life will be a pleasure."

Another lash. The pain was so intense he couldn't help the bellow that escaped his lips.

"When you're gone, little Mer will be mine," Leth whispered in his ear.

Hayjen threw his head back, crashing it into the first mate's face. A satisfying crunch sounded. No one would hurt the little girl.

"You'll regret that," Leth spat. "And so will the little slave."

"I think not," a feminine voice purred.

Hayjen froze. He didn't recognize the voice. Slowly, he turned his neck and stared at the woman perched on the railing. Her shocking magenta eyes met his.

"Let's play a game, shall we?"

Chapter Two

Lilja

Scanning the deck, Lilja took pleasure in the way the crew of Scythian men gaped at her. She doubted they had ever encountered someone like her and lived to tell the tale. No sign of any of the slaves, other than the one tied to the mast. They must be below. The tall warrior with the whip drew her attention as he turned towards her. His smile was sensual with a cruel edge. He was dangerous—she could see it in the way his body moved and the intelligent glint in his black eyes. She assumed he was one of the warlord's older creations, a warrior bred and altered to be perfect. She had to be careful with this one.

Cocking her head, she shifted so her naked thigh peeked out of her skirt, the moonlight highlighting her pale flesh. Would he take the bait? Most of the warlord's warriors had so much testosterone running through their bodies that they couldn't help themselves. The ringleader's eyes followed her movement and relaxed a fraction, his gaze running over her exposed skin.

Men. They were so easy to distract sometimes.

She held back her disgust when he licked his lips. "It's not safe for you to be wandering around at this time of night." His cronies laughed around him.

How unoriginal. Did they have a book that they all memorized? One with cliché lines to use on women? She shook her head, and allowed a smoky chuckle to emerge. Time to get down to business. "No, I assure you I am quite safe. It is your own health you should be worrying about."

"I highly doubt that." The ringleader glanced at his men before meeting her eyes with a challenge. "You are quite alone. I, on the other hand, am surrounded."

Surrounded. How appropriate. He was surrounded, he just didn't know it yet. Her crew was as silent as the night and just as deadly. Little did he know that they lurked in the shadows. There would be blood shed tonight, but it would not be hers. Her eyes sharpened when he took a step towards her.

"I feel like I need to remind you that you are trespassing on my ship, Sirenidae whore." The

Scythian leader spat.

So he knew what she was. Good. She wanted him to know it was a creature he deemed unworthy of life that had bested him. It would make her victory that much sweeter.

"Do you know what we do with your kind? We use them and then toss them back to the Leviathan where they belong."

The threat hardly registered. She'd heard worse over the years from indoctrinated Scythians. Their hate for her kind was legendary. Anything different was condemned. That was part of the reason the Sirenidae disappeared into the sea hundreds of years ago. Scythia was becoming too powerful, too dangerous, too radical. Lilja's eyes narrowed as his eyes scanned her again, lingering on areas he had no business looking at. His beastly nature was showing itself.

"But I'll make an exception for you. I like my women a little wild with some fight."

She slipped to the deck in a fluid movement and leaned against the rail, fighting to keep her disgust from her face. "When I spoke of games, that wasn't quite what I had in mind."

He shifted and Lilja tensed, knowing what would happen. In the space of a heartbeat he was pressed against her, his arms clasping the rail, caging her in.

She wasn't a short woman, but he made her feel downright delicate. The warrior was uncommonly large. Her jaw tensed when he dipped, his lips by her ear. She hated this part.

"What kind of games would you like to play?" he hissed.

She ran her hands up his huge chest and ignored the flare of heat she saw in his eyes. Her fingers fluttered along his collarbone, drawing designs as his breathing became labored. Lilja met his eyes and tipped up onto her toes. He wrapped his hands around her waist and dipped his head so she could speak to him. She met the eyes of a burly man strapped to the mast as she whispered in the warrior's ear. "Lesson number one of hand-to-hand combat. Never let your opponent get too close." She pressed at the base of his skull, using the death touch. His body went slack and crashed to the deck.

There was a beat of silence before the other Scythians charged her. Lilja reached into the folds of her sarong and pulled her twin cutlasses from their sheaths. Her men exploded from the dark and scrambled up the sides of the ship, cutting Scythians down as she cleared a path to the slave tied to the mast. Several Scythians rushed into the fray from below deck, only to be mowed down, despite their biological advantages.

Lilja eyed the slave's back and grimaced. His flesh was laced with old scars and healing lashes that the new beating had ripped open—it was literally cut to ribbons. Would he survive such injuries? Lilja doubted it, but she wouldn't leave him there to die tied to the mast. She slipped to the side and jerked back as his ice blue eyes clashed with hers. Pain, hate, and rage simmered in them, just waiting to be released. She leaned forward until their noses almost touched. "I am going to release you. Don't attack me." Lilja gave him a warning look before straightening and slicing open the ropes.

"Behind you," his hoarse voice warned.

She ducked and slashed her cutlass across the calf of the Scythian attacking her. He bellowed and fell to his knees still viciously stabbing at her. Lilja deftly avoided his attacks and danced around him. She darted in and smashed her pommel against the back of his head. All fight went out of the giant as he crashed to the deck. Breathing hard, she pulled her eyes from the defeated Scythian to the carnage around her. Scythians littered the deck, moaning and cursing. Her gaze swept over her crew as they took care of any stragglers. Female shrieks, curses, and crying floated through the air announcing the arrival of the other slaves. Bedraggled women and girls poured out of the stairway led by her men. From the corner of her eye, she saw the male slave shuffle painfully over to the group.

"Hayjen!" a little girl with silvery blond hair cried.

Lilja's eyes zeroed in on the child. Mer. They had found her niece. She glanced at Lilja as she wrapped her arms around the male, causing him to cry out and fall to his knees. Lilja's heart pinched when there wasn't any recognition in Mer's eyes. This was the price of her ignorance and morals. Her family. Her niece should know her, but life wasn't always fair.

She cocked her head, intrigued as the group of girls surrounded the man, offering help. Curious. Every woman gazed at him with concern or adoration. She'd seen looks like those before. Hero worship.

"Are you okay, Hayjen?" One of the girls asked.

"I'm okay, Lera."

"Captain Femi?"

She pulled her attention from the spectacle and raised an eyebrow in question at her first mate Blair. "Yes?"

"Everyone on the ship is accounted for, Captain."

"Thank you."

"What would you have us do with all the slaves?"

"That's the question of the night, isn't it, Blair?" What would they do with the other slaves? Their priorities were to retrieve the little girl, return her to her parents, and ruin a Scythian ship. It wasn't until they had spotted the ship that they'd found out it was holding more kidnapped victims than just her niece. "I will deal with it."

Lilja strode to the group of slaves, halting five paces away. "Do you have a leader among you?" her voice cut through the dark night.

The man hefted himself up, a groan of pain slipping out. He wiped at the sweat beading across his forehead and pushed his shoulders back, the corner of his eyes pinching. "I am."

He must have been in an inordinate amount of pain, yet he stood before her like a warrior. Lilja was impressed. The little Sirenidae girl placed her little hand on his large, weathered one.

"I have a few questions," Lilja stated.

"I am sure you do, but how about you answer mine first?" His ice blue eyes narrowed. "What do you want with my people, pirate?"

"Nothing, actually." Pirate. She loved being called a pirate. "I hadn't planned on a bushel of slaves being on this ship when I attacked. We love to cause the Scythians grief when we can. I fully intended to burn the ship." The women gasped. "But rest assured, I don't plan on leaving you on this ship while it burns. While I may be in the business of thievery, mayhem, and vengeance, I am not in the business of murder.

So if you'd be so kind as to board my ship The Sirenidae without carrying on, I would be much obliged to you." Lilja didn't think his eyes could get much colder, but they did.

"And what are you planning on doing with us once we board your ship? Do you have plans to sell us? Because I can tell you, we won't go down without a fight if that is the case."

Lilja eyed him. "A prideful one, aren't you? You're beaten and broken, yet you stand before me with dignity and demand answers. That takes courage." She dipped her chin. "I'll answer your questions. I despise slavery." Lilja jerked her thumb over her shoulder. "Just ask my crew, most of whom I have rescued from some form of slavery. It's a vile, evil practice that I have no aspirations to indulge in. I plan to drop you safely on Aermian soil, hopefully to never see you again."

He studied her, his eyes moving over her face like a physical touch. "What is your name?"

"Captain Lilja Femi at your service," she said as she dipped into a bow. "And to whom am I speaking?"

"Hayjen Fiori."

"Well, Hayjen Fiori, what say you?"

He looked at the women around him before turning back to her. "Do I have your solemn oath none of these women will be harmed in any way, and all will be returned to their families?"

"I promise to give them means to reach their families and that they will come to no harm, but getting to their families will be their responsibility."

Lilja placed her hand on the railing to watch the sea as Hayjen whispered to the women surrounding him. She turned back around when the whispering subsided. Hayjen dipped his chin, his mouth pulled tight by pain. "We accept your terms."

"Great!" She slapped her hands together, and smiled at the women warmly. "Blair!" Her second in command started moving in her direction. "Blair will organize you so that we can move you safely to our ship The Sirenidae. If any of you need a healer, please let Blair know. May I speak with you for a moment in private, Hayjen?"

He nodded and moved towards her in jerky movements, eyeing her like she was a Leviathan circling him. "Are any of the children yours?" Her question surprised him. He jerked and glanced over his shoulder at Mer, who was sitting on a barrel watching them.

"Yes, the little one with the blond hair."

Lilja pursed her lips. He was lying. Why? Did he know Mer's worth? "I have to say, she looks nothing like you."

"She's adopted."

"I see."

Hayjen glared at her and leaned forward. "Your tone says otherwise. Unless you are going to accuse me of something, keep your questions and opinions to yourself. Mer is *mine.*"

"Now, now, I think you have the wrong impression of me." Lilja gave him her most sultry smile. "I've implied—" a whisper of a sound caught her attention. She turned just as the Scythian ringleader plowed into her, knocking all three of them over the balcony and into the black waters.

Lilja breathed a sigh of relief as the water caressed her skin.

Home.

She opened her eyes, seeing through the dark water clearly. The Scythian struggled to the surface but Hayjen sunk deeper, blood from his back swirling around in crimson streaks.

That wasn't good.

Leviathan could smell blood from hundreds of feet away.

She dove deeper, sucking in a painful breath of water as her lungs closed and her gills opened. Lilja pushed through the transition, reaching Hayjen as her skin began to tingle. The Leviathan were here. Lilja wrapped her arms around the male and lifted her head, her white hair floating in front of her, giving her glimpses of the sleek black bodies circling. Baring her teeth, she hummed a warning tone. One darted in, its sharp white teeth gleaming in the dark water. She snapped her teeth at the beast, causing it to retreat into the circle. Normally they wouldn't dare test a Sirenidae, but when a meal was in sight, they tended to get excited. The largest of the finned creatures faced her and swam until it was within arm's length. The alpha. She met its black eyes and stared it down until its nose dipped. Lilja reached her hand out, allowing the Leviathan the choice to make friends. It eyed her and then bumped its nose into her palm.

Relief washed through her. There wouldn't be a fight for dominance tonight.

The Leviathan turned its attention to the Scythian man fighting the waves above. A series of hums drifted through the water, making the hair on her arms stand up. Their hunting song always gave her chills. Lilja propelled herself and Hayjen to the surface. She braced herself for her first breath. Transitioning from sea breathing to air breathing hurt. Lilja choked and coughed as she expelled water from her lungs. Her chest burned and tears came to her eyes. She shuddered as she coughed more water and began hauling them to the side of the ship where a net swayed.

"Captain! You need to get out of the water now!" Blair shouted, fear tingeing his voice.

Lilja looked over her shoulder at what had caught his attention. The Leviathan were circling the Scythian, taking playful nips. They always liked to play with their food. It was the fins following her, however, that must have caused her first mate's panic. Lilja picked up her pace, ignoring the curious beasts following her. They were probably hoping she would give up her prey.

Not today, beasties.

A soul-shattering scream erupted behind her, making her wince. No one deserved to die like that. The scream cut off in abrupt silence. It was time to get out before a feeding frenzy started. Even she wasn't stupid enough to be in the water when they went crazy. Lilja latched onto the net, desperately holding on to Hayjen. "Pull us up!" she yelled.

Her arms screamed as she clung to the large man. His weight was almost too much to bear, but the sight of the dark creatures now directly below her was all she needed to help maintain her hold on him. Her crew heaved one last time and pulled them over the railing. She coughed up the rest of the sea water and pushed onto her hands and knees.

"Depths below, Captain. You smell so damn good."

Hell. The sea water activated her Lure. What was meant to be a protection for her kind, only caused her trouble. Her poor crew couldn't help but be drawn to her. It was chemistry.

"It's the Lure. Step back and the effect will lessen." She blinked the salt water out of her eyes and glanced over at Hayjen, eyes widening. "Get him off his back!"

Blair dropped to his knees and pressed on the man's chest. "We have to get the water from his lungs first or he won't survive."

Her first mate pushed on his chest over and over before Hayjen's lips sputtered and he spit up water. Blair quickly turned him to his side, blood and sea water pouring everywhere. Hayjen yelled and went limp.

"Is he okay?" she demanded, gaping at his back. It was a bloody mess.

"He's unconscious. We need to get him off this hunk of wood and onto our ship."

Lilja nodded, never taking her eyes off his back. The pain must have been excruciating. *Depths below*, the man had suffered, and all the open flesh had been subjected to the salty sea water. He was lucky he'd passed out. At least that way he'd feel no pain.

Chapter Three

Hayjen

Stars above, his body bloody hurt. He blinked at the colorful bedding beneath his cheek. Where was he? Hayjen moved to get up and yelped, falling back to the bed. He breathed hard as pain and nausea washed through him. That was stupid. He put his nose into the blankets and attempted to breathe through the pain assaulting him. Vaguely, he registered citrus and sea salt.

"What the hell did you do?" a smoky voice asked.

Hayjen jerked painfully, and turned his neck to spot pirate Captain Femi glaring at him as she bore down on him.

"You opened your wounds back up," she scolded.

His nose twitched when her green silk dress

brushed his nose. How cliché—a pirate wearing silk.

"I heard that, you ungrateful brute."

He had said that out loud? He must be addled. "Sorry."

"Hmmmm…"

Pain bit him. "Damn it, that hurt." What was she doing? Where was Mer?

"Stop being such a sissy, and hold still. You would think I was torturing you or something."

"Then stop poking me."

"I wouldn't be poking you if you hadn't ripped open your wounds."

"Where's Mer?"

"Behave and I'll tell you. Hold still. I'm putting seaweed on your back."

"Seaweed?" She was talking in circles.

"Among other things."

"Mer?"

"She's fine."

"That's not an answer."

She remained silent as she worked.

Hayjen scowled, guessing that would be the only answer he received. Bloody pirates. He gritted his teeth as she worked, channeling his pain to focus on the room he was in. There wasn't much to see but a doorway out to what he assumed to be her study. A large desk made from blue- green wood dominated the middle of the space. Two large bookcases stuffed to the brim with books bracketed a bay window with a window seat. Colorful pillows spilled across the seat in a disheveled, homey way. So the pirate liked to read. Interesting. His only experiences with pirates had been with illiterate thieves who were in need of baths. Speaking of baths, Hayjen caught a whiff of himself and cringed. He stunk. "How long have I been sleeping?"

"You've been in and out for four days."

He stiffened. Four days? Who had taken care of the women, and Mer?

"Calm yourself. Mer and the girls are fine."

"Forgive me if I don't believe you until I witness it with my own eyes." Like he would believe the words of a person who made it her career to steal from others.

Her hands paused. "I made a promise."

"Not everyone keeps their word."

"True." A breath. "Mer, I know you are listening at the door. Come in!"

The door was flung open and little feet slapped against the wooden floor. Despite his pain, Hayjen smiled at the sound. Mer never walked anywhere—she ran. She skidded to a stop in front of his nose and dropped to her knees. His worry loosened a bit as he saw her healthy, precious face. Mer flung her arm around his neck and squeezed; his back pulled, but it was worth it for a hug. "I missed you too, Mer."

She pulled back, her little eyes filling with tears. "I was so scared, Hayjen. The Leviathan almost got you, and then you stopped breathing, and then you wouldn't wake up!" she cried.

"Shhh..." Hayjen soothed, wishing he could hold her in his arms. "I'm okay. Captain Femi has taken great care of me. I will be better before you know it."

Mer's eyes slid to the silent woman tending his back. "She's alright."

The captain sniggered.

"What have you been up to while I was sleeping? Did you behave yourself?"

Mer met his eyes and nodded her head so enthusiastically her hair tumbled from her bun. "I helped the cook make soup, I fixed a net with Blair, and I even was able to go for a swim with Lilja."

Hayjen's eyes narrowed, his hackles raising. Why would the captain take time to swim with a little girl? Why take an interest in Mer? One thing was for sure—he didn't like it. Not one bit.

"Tell him what we discovered," the captain hinted with a smile.

Mer's eyes sparkled with excitement. She practically vibrated on her toes. "We found an oyster bed! Look!" She pulled up a thin, silver chain hidden beneath the neck of her dress, exposing a small cage encasing a pearl the same soft lilac color as Mer's eyes. "I got to pick the oyster and Lilja dove for it. When we opened it, this was what was inside!"

"It's beautiful," Hayjen remarked. It didn't matter what age a girl was—they all loved trinkets from the sea. He eyed the pearl with suspicion. What was Captain Femi up to? The Scythians had had an unhealthy obsession with the girl—maybe the pirates had a similar interest. He lifted his eyes to Mer's. She was looking at him with innocent joy. Maybe it was just a gift and he was being paranoid.

No, if he had been paranoid, he wouldn't have been caught by the Scythians. He was using good sense, and his sense told him that Captain Femi was an edgy character.

Hayjen sighed when his back began to tingle—not in a bad way, but merely from numbness. Blessedly without pain. His muscles relaxed and he practically melted into the bed with a relieved smile. "I am glad you had a good time."

A bell rang loudly, surprising Hayjen. "What was that?'

Shooting to her feet, Mer plopped a kiss on his forehead. "It's lunch time," she said before darting out the door.

"She has a lot of energy," Lilja commented.

That was an understatement. She never stopped moving. "Yep." His eyelids drooped, much to his frustration—hadn't he had enough sleep? The pirate continued her ministrations. Hayjen blinked slowly. Had she drugged him? "What did you say was in that salve?"

The captain pushed off the bed and moved into his line of sight. "I didn't."

"Did you drug me?" he slurred.

Captain Femi threw her head back, laughing. Her silvery white braid tumbling down her back. Her eyes met his with humor glimmering in their depths. "If I had drugged you, you would know it." She chuckled, and began cleaning up her supplies. "It is a family recipe."

He still didn't believe her, but he found himself muttering, "Fair enough." His own mum had secret family recipes.

Hayjen took the moment to really look at Captain Femi. The dark night he had met her hadn't done her shocking beauty justice. Her silvery white hair was in a thick braid tossed over her shoulder, emphasizing her long, graceful arms and body. She was tall, but still shorter than he was. What intrigued him the most, though, were her odd magenta eyes. He'd never seen anyone with that color before. Between her striking eyes, shiny hair, and unique coloring, she made quite the image. She paused in her cleaning and raised a brow in question. Hayjen coughed and offered her an appreciative smile. "Thank you for taking care of Mer, and my back."

Captain Femi waved a hand at him. "Think nothing of it. Soon enough you will be off my ship." With that parting remark, she sauntered out of the room.

She was a character.

One he wasn't sure he could trust.

Hayjen closed his eyes just for a moment and sunk into a painless sleep.

Sleek black beasts circled him. He was going to die in a watery grave. The pale moonlight above shimmered through the waves like it was saying goodbye. Hayjen wanted to let go. He was tired, his body hurt. Just as he closed his eyes, something slammed into him causing his eyes to spring open. Smooth, pale female arms wrapped around his chest as shimmering white hair swirled in the currents cocooning the woman and himself. He smiled at the idea of dying in the arms of a beautiful woman.

What a way to go.

It was only when her hair parted that fear squeezed him. Huge Leviathan circled them, just waiting to attack their prey. If he could have moved, he would have. Now the beautiful woman holding him would die as well. His heart flew to his throat as the largest of the Leviathan swam at them, halting within arm's reach. Its jagged teeth were so close they could tear into his flesh. Its eyes were the worst. No color—just black soulless orbs. Hayjen wanted to scream when the pale hand clutching him reached out to the immense sea creature. He waited for the Leviathan to tear into her, but to his surprise, it bumped its snout into her palm and hummed before backing away.

His body began to cut quickly through the water. How was he moving? He wasn't swimming—he couldn't move his arms. Idly, he gave up trying to figure out the phenomenon and watched the monstrous creature's tail above them. His head bobbed, giving him a glimpse of the woman carrying him. Fascinated, he stared at her neck. Gills, she had gills. Then everything went black.

He jerked awake to find sweat pouring down his face.

What was that? he thought.

He'd had nightmares before, but nothing like that. He shivered, the hair on his arms rising as he recalled the empty black eyes of the Leviathan watching him. It had felt so real, like it had really happened. Hayjen placed his forehead on the coverlet and breathed deeply, trying to center himself and forget the nightmare.

"Are you alright?" The captain's smoky voice floated through the air.

Hayjen craned his neck to watch her glide into the room. Moonlight caressed her loose silvery hair making it seem like it was glowing. She looked ethereal, otherworldly. He blinked. She looked a lot like the woman from his dream. Odd. The mind was a curious thing.

"Hayjen?" she questioned, stopping by the side of the bed.

"Just a nightmare," he replied, still trying to shake off the dream. Stars above, it had felt real, like a memory.

"Oh."

He squinted at her, still seeing her in his mind with gills. People didn't have gills, but still he found himself wishing her hair wasn't covering her neck. His brow furrowed as he tried to remember exactly what had happened after the Scythian had knocked them into the water. He came up blank. "What happened once the Scythian knocked us into the water?" he asked, peering up at the pirate.

Surprise flickered across her face at his question. "We hit the water. Luckily for us, I was able to grab you and pull you into the net."

That couldn't be it. The water had been swarming with Leviathan. "And the Leviathan?"

"Too preoccupied with the Scythian."

He frowned. Leviathan were known to go into a frenzy at the smell of blood. He had been ripped to shreds after his beating, covered in blood. How had he survived? The beasts were wickedly fast—they couldn't have outswam them.

"You hit your head when we fell."

That explained the memory loss, but not how he'd survived. Nothing made sense, but her story rang false in his ears even so. What was she hiding?

The captain shifted on her feet, and brushed her hair over her shoulder. His eyes zeroed in on her neck. No gills. He was an idiot. A person having gills made no sense. It was just a dream, nothing more.

"Well, I'll let you rest."

Hayjen stared at the doorway as she swept out of the room, disappearing into her office. He needed more rest. Or he was going crazy. It was probably the latter.

He woke up with a smile. His back itched and ached,

but he wasn't in excruciating pain. That was something to be happy about. Gingerly, Hayjen stretched and pushed himself from the bed. His whole body revolted, so it took a couple times to sit up. Dizziness assailed him and the room blurred. Taking deep breaths, he focused on the flower rug beneath his bare feet. So feminine. The captain was an interesting study in opposites.

Once the room stopped spinning and his lightheadedness had receded, he braced his hands on the bed and stumbled to his feet, nearly braining himself against the doorway as he tried to catch his balance. The bloody ship wasn't helping as it bobbed through the waves.

Carefully, using the walls and anything he could find, he moved through Captain Femi's study and opened the door. The hallway was dark, but he could see sunlight at the end. Hayjen moved slowly towards it, hands pressing against the opposite walls, and paused just out of the light, breathless at the view.

The girls were laughing and working together with *real* smiles on their faces. Hayjen could count on one hand how many times each of them had smiled in their time together on the Scythian slave ship. He eyed the rest of the crew working. They darted glances at the girls but held neither malice nor lust, just curiosity. Many men would take advantage of an abused weak woman, yet none of the men were. Captain Femi ran a tight ship.

The ship rolled, causing him to stumble and slip into view. Mer saw him first and let out a squeal of delight before sprinting to him. He braced himself for the impact, knowing it would hurt.

A man with a warrior's build he vaguely remembered snatched Mer around the waist and swung her through the air. "Young one, remember that he's hurt. You need to be careful or you will injure him more."

Mer nodded emphatically, her lilac eyes round. "Okay, Blair."

Blair.

Captain Femi's first mate.

Blair dropped Mer to her feet and she covered the distance between them in a much more sedate manner. She wrapped her pale arms around his leg and gave him the smile he had come to love. "Missed you."

He brushed her unruly white-blonde hair out of her face, soaking in the happiness she wore like a cloak. "The same." Hayjen lifted his head and met the dark brown eyes of the first mate. He didn't look like an evil man, but one could never be sure. His eyes dropped to Mer and back to the first mate. The little girl had an uncanny sense of character. If she liked the man, then he was probably okay. He jerked his chin towards Mer. "Thank you."

Blair studied him, then nodded once before turning and barking at the crew about some mess. A man of very little words apparently. A cough pulled his attention from the first mate. His eyes widened at the group that surrounded him. His women surrounded him with various smiles, some thankful, others happy and excited, some relieved.

"We're happy you've recovered," Lera remarked softly from the middle of the group.

Hayjen gaped. He'd never heard Lera speak before. Snapping his mouth closed he asked, "Have you been taken care of?"

"We have."

He looked over the group of women with a smile. "I knew we would escape."

"You said we would, and here we are. Thank you, Hayjen. You have made sacrifices for all of us, and we will never forget your kindness. We are all in your debt."

"Never." And he meant it. He would do it all over again to protect them from those monsters. No one deserved the life the Scythians had planned for them.

Of course, his stomach had to ruin the moment by growling loudly.

Lera grinned, shocking him again. "The food is incredible."

His stomach growled again.

Mer tugged on his hand, turning his attention back to her.

"Come eat what I helped Cook make!"

He grinned at the thought of Mer bothering the poor cook to death. "Have you been a bother?"

"Nope, it was my job. Captain Femi says if I want to be like her when I grow up, I must have a job. I like to eat, so I thought making food with Cook was a good idea."

"Indeed." Hayjen lifted his head and locked eyes with Captain Femi who was watching their exchange with interest. He wasn't comfortable with her, but he owed her his life, and the lives of the women. He jerked his chin at her in acknowledgement. She arched a brow with a smirk before returning the gesture, then dismissed him. He watched her speak with her first mate for a moment, absently noting she was wearing leather pants. Surprisingly, they were just as sensual on her as her intriguing knotted dresses. Hayjen scowled and turned to follow the insistent tugging of Mer's hand.

Best to not be admiring something he didn't trust.

She screamed danger.

He didn't need danger, he needed a good meal.

Chapter Four

Lilja

"He doesn't trust you."

Lilja turned to Blair with an arched brow. "You don't say?"

Her first mate rolled his dark brown eyes. "I just mean you should be careful. What he went through ruins a person. He won't be right in the head for a long time."

"He's not broken."

"No, he's not, but he won't be healed for a long time, no matter how many salves you apply to his back."

She blinked at her friend. He was always very astute when it came to emotions. He could read almost anyone, but he was hard to read himself. Even after spending years together, he still surprised her.

"I just wanted to help him."

Blair slipped his hand into hers and squeezed, then let go. "You want to help everyone, and that's what I love about you, but you can't fix a person."

"That's where you and I disagree." Lilja gestured between the two of them. "I believe we've helped heal each other."

He sighed. "Yes, but we're different. We were both shoved together into a situation that bonded us for life. That man is not your partner, but a project, someone you want to save. He will distract you from what's important, Lil."

She didn't like it, but she trusted her old friend. "I won't ever forget what's most important, Blair. I won't let another woman be experimented on by the Scythians."

"I know, Lil. I know."

She touched her first mate's shoulder. "No one will ever have to experience what we suffered."

Blair cupped her face. "Never again."

"Never again," she echoed.

Blair dropped his hand and stared out at the sea. "So how are we going to return Mer to her family? Hayjen will not let us take her—if we steal her, he will come for her. He loves her like she is his own."

"As does she," Lilja grimaced. "It was hard enough to explain to Mer why she couldn't speak about the sea."

"It's only a matter of time before she says something." Her friend glanced at her. "She's only five. It will slip." Blair crossed his arms and cocked his head. "You've been too careless since we've rescued the slaves. You should have let him die that night, but you exposed yourself by singing to the Leviathan. Then when we pulled you up, your gills were uncovered. You can't risk yourself like that."

Her eyes narrowed at his chastising tone. "What did you expect me to do? That Scythian scum knocked me into the ocean, forcing my gills open. Whether or not I saved Hayjen didn't matter. I was still exposed."

Blair's brow furrowed. "I know, I am frustrated that you were put in that position in the first place, and on edge with strangers on our ship that know nothing of the secret our crew hides. It would only take one slip, one mistake, and you would be in danger."

"I've lived this way a long time, Blair. This is nothing new."

He blew out a breath. "I know, but you would put the girls in danger as well. Your crew chose to take the burden and risk of your secret on themselves, but the girls did not. You need to wear your wrap when you swim."

"That's fair." It would kill her if something happened to the innocents because of what she hid.

A quiet moment passed as they admired the rolling deep blue waves frothing and swirling around the ship. "How long until we reach land?"

"We'll reach the cove near Sanee in three weeks," Blair replied.

"When will we meet with Mer's parents?"

"In two."

Lilja pursed her lips. "That's going to be a problem."

Her first mate laughed. "You don't say?"

"We'll have to lock him up."

"He won't like that."

"I'm sure he won't."

"He'll fight."

"Not if I drug him."

Blair glanced at her from the corner of his eye and sniggered at her devious expression. "He has no idea what he did when he accepted your help."

"I don't know what you mean." Lilja sniffed. "I am an upstanding individual."

"You are a fraud, a thief, and a pirate."

"I only steal from bad people."

"Still doesn't make it right."

"I don't see you complaining."

"I made my peace with what I am and what you

are a long time ago."

"You're not so bad." She bumped her shoulder against Blair's.

"I used to be."

The air around them grew heavy at his statement. "Not anymore," Lilja said carefully, lowering her voice. "The person you were doesn't exist anymore. You made the choice to be better."

"I can't change how I was created."

"No, but the warlords experiments were out of your control. How you were raised was out of your control. But how you acted once you realized what the warlord was doing was in your control, and you made the right decision."

"It doesn't change what I've done."

No, it didn't, but you couldn't change the past. "What matters is that you feel remorse for what you've done. You now know it was wrong to take women and breed them. You changed the way you think and act. That is what matters. You've made amends."

He gestured to the ship angrily. "This? Pirating Scythian ships?"

"We're saving lives."

"Something needs to change, Lil. We aren't changing a damn thing. Damien is still ruling and experimenting."

She stabbed a finger towards the galley. "Those girls we just rescued are proof that we are making a change. Each and every one of their lives were saved because of our actions."

"It's not enough."

"It has to be for now."

He glanced at her. "We need to know what is going on inside the borders."

Her throat tightened. She knew where he was leading with this conversation. They had argued about it time after time. "We can't go back in."

"No, you can't go back in."

"You'll die if you do."

"Maybe, maybe not."

A part of her knew he was right. They wouldn't overturn a corrupt warlord by pirating his ships. "We'll cross that bridge when we come to it."

"The bridge is looming in front of us."

"You need to let the hurt and guilt go, or it will eat you up inside. Entering Scythian lands won't make that disappear."

Blair's smile was bittersweet. "It's not easy, or simple."

"No, it's not," Lilja stated bluntly. "I should know."

He met her eyes, a grave expression on his face. "It wasn't your fault."

Her breath seized at the reminder, and her eyes

dropped to the deck. "I should have been more careful."

Blair slipped his hand into hers, holding tight. "Look at me."

Lilja lifted her eyes and met Blair's gaze—his eyes the deep brown of chocolate.

"It was not your fault. You did everything right. You protected her and yourself. Sometimes these things happen."

"It was an accident," she whispered, never taking her eyes off him. "I shouldn't have fought him."

Blair's face hardened, looking like he was cut from stone. "No, even if you hadn't fought that monster, Gem wouldn't have been safe."

Soul-wrenching pain stabbed her. Gem. Blair rarely said her name. Lilja blinked back her tears, refusing to cry. "I wish...I wish things were different. I—" she hiccupped.

Blair gave her a sad smile that echoed her own pain. "As do I."

That simple statement gave Lilja a measure of peace. She wasn't alone. Gem would never be forgotten; her memories would live on in their hearts.

Her first mate blew out a breath and released her hand, grabbing the rail. "You know, you could meet a man and settle down to have a wonderful family."

"Nothing could replace Gem," she barked.

He glanced at her, lips thin. "That's not what I meant. I know you desire a family, and yet you stay on this ship crusading."

She pressed her lips together, moved to Blair's side, and leaned against the rail. It wasn't something she was going to discuss today. "I could say the same of you," she deflected.

"Family life is not for me; the sea is my mistress."

"I beg to differ—you would make a wonderful father."

The corner of his mouth tipped upwards. "Are you saying you fancy me, Lil? You want to have my children?"

Lilja studied him, ignoring his teasing tone. She leaned forward and kissed his cheek. "You are the one person I can depend on in the world. I have no intentions of marrying, but if I did, you would be the first person I'd call upon."

Blair brushed his thumb across the top of her hand. "And I you." He glanced up, peering through his black lashes at her. "I've no plans for that kind of life, but if you asked for marriage and a child, I would give that to you. I love you."

They were a sad pair, the two of them. Both broken and scarred. Their experiences had bound them in ways most people would never be able to understand. They loved each other, but they weren't in love with each other. Blair was the only family she had. "You know I love you."

Blair straightened and flashed her a smile. "Such heavy subjects today."

"It's having Mer aboard. I wish I could tell her who I am."

"There's no reason why you cannot."

"I have every reason. It's enough to be her friend."

A soft smile lit her friend's face. "She breathes life into the people she's around."

"I wish I could bottle it up."

"You would make a fortune off it."

Lilja sniggered. "Just like a pirate. Always thinking about profit." A wicked smile danced across Blair's handsome face, making him look like a true pirate with his black hair, dark eyes, and sea-stained leather.

"I live to loot."

"That's a bad line," she accused.

Blair winked, and glanced over her shoulder. "Higgins isn't cleaning a damn thing, that bag of lazy bones." He brushed a kiss on her cheek and strode away, barking at Higgins.

She tipped her head back, basking in the warm sun. Down in the deep, Sirenidae didn't experience the sun. When she had first come above, the sun had burned her something awful, but after a time, her skin began to build a tolerance and absorb the rays, turning her pale coloring to a soft golden color. Still not tan like her crew, but at least she wasn't the color of a dead fish. In the deep, the dark blues complimented pale skin, but in the harsh light of day it was odd.

Lilja cracked her neck and decided she needed to make friends. If Hayjen didn't trust her, it was going to be a long couple of weeks. She spun and followed the delicious smells of the kitchen. She sauntered in, smiling as the room quieted and many of the women's eyes followed her. Stopping in front of the cook, the thin man who created food that could tempt anyone's palate, she smiled. "What do we have today?"

His thin mustache lifted as he smiled. "Soup, and a hearty bread, Captain."

"Mmmm," she hummed as he doled out her lunch. Lilja thanked him and moved to an open spot among the slave group. She smiled at everyone and ignored their stares as she began to eat. They weren't used to her, but they had warmed up. A little body plopped down next to her, almost knocking over her soup.

"Mer!" a deep voice scolded. "Watch what you are doing."

Lilja peeked at Mer looking properly chastised

and grinned at her, letting her know it was okay. "That's alright, no harm done."

The little girl's lilac eyes looked up at her with excitement bubbling just under the surface. "Do you like it? I helped Cook make it."

"It's delicious. You did a fine job."

Mer leaned forward and gestured to Lilja to do the same. Lilja cocked her head so the little girl could speak in her ear.

"What makes it so good is the secret ingredient. Cook says the secret ingredient is love. I put lots of love into the soup."

Lilja grinned at Mer. "I can tell. Only love would taste so good!"

"You did a fine job," the quiet woman she'd come to know as Lera spoke.

"How are you today, Lera?" she asked.

The mousy woman gave her a sweet smile. "I am well, thanks to you."

She waved a hand at Lera. "All I did was provide the vessel for you to escape on. You kept yourself alive and whole on a Scythian slaver. That's extraordinary." And it was.

"Many of us would have died if it weren't for Hayjen."

So that explained the worshipful looks the girls cast at the burly man.

Lilja finally looked at the man who hadn't stopped staring at her since she walked through the galley doors. His eyes still shocked her. They were such an ice blue that it felt like if you got too close, you would be cold. She'd never seen eyes like his. Ironic really—he had probably never seen eyes like hers either. He broke their stare off and looked to Lera.

"Anyone else would have helped." Hayjen glanced around the group. "It was your care for each other and your determination to stay strong that kept you alive."

Lilja observed the reaction of the women around him. Most of them stared at him like he held the moon. He was a natural leader; he was humble, kind, fierce, and self-sacrificing. The women were lucky that he had been captured with them.

She felt eyes on her and glanced at a girl around the age of 15 staring at her. Lilja smiled and raised a brow. The girl colored and dropped her eyes to her lap. "Was there something you wanted to ask?" The murmurs halted as the girl turned a bright shade of red. "It's okay to speak to me."

The girl's eyes darted from the slave leader to Lilja, and back to her lap. "I a-am curious about your eyes, my lady."

Lilja snorted. "I am no lady, I am a pirate. Please call me Lilja."

"Lilja," the girl tested.

"What's your name?"

"Beth."

"Well, Beth," Lilja leaned forward, "I was born with these eyes." She crossed her eyes, making some of the women giggle around her. "Do you like the color?"

"They're pretty," Beth commented.

"They're not pretty." Hayjen's deep voice rumbled through the room. "They're striking and exotic."

She ignored his comment and focused on Beth. "That's nice of you to say, but I would love to have beautiful hazel eyes like yours. They remind me of a forest at autumn time."

Beth tucked a hair behind her ear, blushing. "Thank you, Lilja."

Lilja lounged on the pillow behind her, and eyed the girls. "It's interesting that we admire others' beauty but we rarely see it in ourselves. Why do you think we do that?"

"Because we live with the flaws every day," a girl named Jess spoke.

"Ah, but what makes them flaws? Who told you that they were flaws?"

"My mum used to say my hair looked like yellow straw instead of silk." Jess brushed her thick blond hair out of her face.

Beth pointed at her own cheeks. "Boys made fun of my freckles."

"Exactly." Lilja sat up. "Others belittled things about your body so that now you look at it in a negative light. Don't buy in to what they say. You only have one body. Love it and take care of it. Their opinions only influence you if you let them." She stood and turned in a circle. "What do you see?"

"Sex and grace," Lera blurted.

Lilja nodded and met the girl's eyes. "At one time, others condemned me and ridiculed me for it. They tried to shame me because of my long limbs and curves. They blamed me for their lust. After a while, I began to believe them, to blame myself and hate my body. All I saw were flaws and sin."

"How did you change?" Beth asked.

"A close friend told me differently. He said if I couldn't accept myself, how could others? That stuck with me. It took time, but eventually I accepted that this is the body I was born with and I began to love it." Dropping into a crouch, she popped a piece of bread into her mouth and chewed, watching as the women absorbed what she had said. She swallowed and continued. "Stop looking for flaws in yourself and embrace the beauty. Each and every one of you are beautiful. I see it, and Hayjen here sees it." Lilja brushed Mer's white blond hair out of her face and stood. "Thank you for the wonderful conversation. I hope to have dinner with you all later."

She turned her back and allowed herself a smile as the conversation continued with them telling each other what they appreciated about each other. Quiet steps followed her. "Yes?" she said, turning abruptly to speak with whoever was following her. Lilja's nose came in contact with a very broad chest. One that smelled extremely pleasing.

She didn't expect that.

Lilja stepped back and tipped her head back to meet his gaze.

Ice eyes.

Stunning face.

Silky hair.

He was too damn attractive.

And moved like a griffin.

She was in trouble.

Chapter Five

Hayjen

Her magenta eyes stared into his with, if he wasn't mistaken, a hint of attraction.

Well, good. She was too bloody beautiful to look at. It would only be fair if she thought he was attractive as well. Hayjen put those thoughts away for later and focused on what he had to say to her.

"Thank you."

She blinked. "You're welcome."

Hayjen hooked a thumb over his shoulder. "For in there." The captain's brilliant smile about blinded him.

"They are wonderful. They deserve to feel that way."

"They are coming back to life."

Her lips pursed as she peered around his

shoulder. "It will be a long time before they will heal. Right now they are running on a high of being free, of being out of danger." Her eyes moved to his. "Soon enough they'll drop and we'll have to keep an eye on them."

"We'll?" he questioned.

"It will be three weeks until we reach the cove near Sanee," she explained.

"So long?" He was hoping to get to his sister sooner than that.

"Scythia is a long way from Sanee, and I am only repeating what my first mate told me."

"Blair?"

"Yes, Blair."

Something in her tone made him pause. There was more feeling in her voice than he would have expected to hear if she was talking about a typical crew member. His heart sank a little bit—despite himself, he was intrigued by this female creature. "I would like to speak with you and your first mate this evening if possible."

"That can be arranged. I will fetch you when dinner is served. Now if you'll excuse me."

She sauntered down the hallway, every step fluid like she was dancing. The captain was great with the girls, but he couldn't help but be suspicious. Was she after something else? Hayjen shook his head. What could she be after? They didn't have anything of value other than their skin. But again his skeptical side reared its head. No one did anything for nothing.

He turned and shuffled down the hallway and into the galley. The gaggle of girls were smiling and complimenting each other. The smile on his face came freely at the sight of their affection and kindness. Carefully, he lowered himself to a large purple pillow surrounding the low table. Beth and Jess cast smiles in his direction but kept on with their conversations.

"What's the first thing you're going to do when you get home?" Jess asked.

"Hug my family," Beth quietly replied.

Hayjen watched them, marveling at how free they looked. He would have done everything in his power to help these women escape, but there at the end he hadn't thought they were going to make it.

A little white-blonde head plopped down next to him and snuggled into his side. Mer. Automatically, he wrapped his arm around her. He stared down at the crown of her head in awe and terror. In awe that such a precious creature was under his care. In terror that he would find her family and have to hand her over. Also, if he was honest, terrified that she was under his care. Hayjen planned on having a family, but not until he passed his thirty-fifth year. That was still seven years down the road. He dropped a kiss on to the sleepy little girl's head and settled on his side to make her more comfortable, even though it pulled on his wounds.

"Love you," Mer whispered.

Hayjen brushed the hair from her face and tipped her chin up, brushing his nose against hers. "Love you too, Mer." She gave him a gap-toothed smile before falling asleep curled into his side. He looked over her sweet face and marveled at her innocence. He glanced up to see most of the women staring at him with affection.

"How did I get so lucky?" he asked no one in particular.

"She's the lucky one. We all are," Lera spoke up.

Hayjen looked down at Mer, watching her eyes flicker behind her lids. "I don't know how to care for her."

"You've done a good enough job so far," whispered a gangly girl named Belle.

"She was almost eaten by Leviathan." The words tasted sour in his mouth.

"But she wasn't," soothed Lera.

"What will I do if I can't find her family?" He looked up at the girls. "I will need to work to support her. Who will stay home and care for her? Teach her? I know nothing of little girls, other than my sister."

"Where is your sister?"

Hayjen's lips thinned. "I don't know. She's unmarried and we've no family. If I wasn't there to provide for her—"He sucked in a breath. "I've been gone for months."

"If she's anything like you, she will be just fine when we return to Aermia. And if you can't find Mer's family, you'll have your sister to help care for her."

That could work, but it felt like Gwen was still a little girl, too. He had raised her after their parents had died, so she'd always be young to him.

Looking around the room, Hayjen asked, "How are you all *really*?"

Belle's brown eyes met his then dropped to the pillow she sat on as she fiddled with a string. "The crew have treated us well, and they feed us." A pause. "The nightmares are still there."

He nodded. "Those I fear will take some time to abate."

"The men are kind," blurted Beth.

Hayjen turned to her with a raised brow.

Her cheeks colored, but she didn't drop her eyes. "They don't look at us with disgust and lust like the slavers did." She shivered slightly. "They don't yell or raise their voices around us. I've never caught any of them gazing at us with anything but curiosity and pity."

"Hmmm..." he hummed.

"The captain assigned us jobs on the second day we were here," Lera spoke. "She said it would help to get back to normal." She shrugged. "When you're busy, you don't have time to dwell on the negatives in your life."

"Have they questioned any of you?" he asked.

"The captain and her first mate have probed, but they haven't interrogated us if that's what you're worried about."

"A kind pirate, go figure," he mumbled.

"Never judge."

"Yes, mum," Hayjen grumbled with a smile.

Lera arched a brow and shook her head at him. "Cheeky devil."

"The captain informed me that it would be three weeks until we reach Aermia."

Silence.

"Well, we've been on a ship for this long, what's another couple of weeks?" Beth remarked. "Plus, some of us don't know what we are returning home to."

His gaze narrowed on the girl. "Will you be in danger?"

She waved a hand. "Nothing like that. I was betrothed before I was taken. I'm not sure I will be when I return."

"He'd be a fool to turn you away."

Her smile was wan. "If only all men had your ideals, Hayjen."

"Then he's not worthy."

"Kind words."

His back decided to protest at his position, causing him to wince. "I think I need to lie down for a bit." Hayjen extracted himself from Mer and stumbled to his feet. Lera adjusted Mer on the pillows and smiled at him.

"We'll watch over her. Rest."

Nodding, he shuffled out of the room, his eyes heavy. Hayjen managed to make it back to his room, ignoring his curiosity to explore the captain's study. He crashed onto the bed. The pain receded. He breathed a sigh of relief and closed his eyes.

Hayjen slept away the afternoon and was surprised when he woke to only a sliver of light glimmering over the horizon. It took a while to pull off his soiled pants, clean up, and don the new clothing left by someone. He laced the billowing white linen shirt loosely around his throat, pleased to find that the cloth didn't irritate his wounds. The brown leather pants fit him perfectly, and he wondered offhandedly how they knew his size. He shrugged it off as not being important.

Now, as he entered the captain's study, he took his time. He shuffled over to the bookshelf, running his fingers along the colorful spines. She loved books— that was clear. His eyes moved to her organized desk—not a thing out of place. So she liked things just so. He filed that away. Color saturated everything he saw. It fit her. Wild color everywhere. Yet somehow they all mixed together in a way that was pleasing.

Finishing his perusal, he left her study and went out onto the deck. Men were scattered everywhere, sitting on barrels or crates. Some nodded to him as he passed them on his way to the rail. He leaned against it, watching the last of the sun's rays disappear. There wasn't anything more beautiful than the sun setting on the ocean. He sucked in a deep breath, savoring the salty crisp air and the symphony of waves crashing against the ship.

Peace.

It had been forever since he felt a measure of peace. After his parents had died, it had always been about feeding and raising Gwen. She was eight years his junior and needed someone to take care of her. Once captured, it became about protecting the girls and Mer. He was weary to his bones. No wonder he had been sleeping for days—he had been sleeping with one eye open most of the time for months. But being here, now, in this moment, there was nothing but the sea breeze rustling his hairs and the waves below him. A smile tugged at his lips as light footsteps moved in his direction.

So much for peace and quiet.

Mer's little hand slipped into his and to his surprise, she stayed silent, staring out at the dark waves. After a while, she shifted into his side to block some of the wind.

"Are you cold?" he asked softly.

"No, I just wanted to hug you. I miss my papa."

Hayjen knelt and pulled her into his arms for a hug. Her little arms wrapped around his neck, her face pressed into his chest. Her statement broke his heart. "We'll find them."

She shook her head. "You won't."

He let go of her and cupped her cheeks, staring into her unique eyes. "I'll search for them. I will look forever if I have to, but while I look for them, will you stay with me?"

Her serious little face searched his. "I'll stay with you, but…you can't find mama and papa."

"Why?" Had the Scythians done something to her parents? Mer rarely spoke of them.

"You can't live in the sea."

His brows furrowed as he stared at her in confusion. Live in the sea? "What do you mean?"

She bit her lip, eyes darting around the deck. "It's a secret."

"What is, baby girl?"

"Mama and papa said to never tell anyone, because it would put me I danger."

What in the bloody hell? Hayjen took a calming

breath. "Have I ever hurt you, Mer?"

"No. You love me."

"That's right, and I will never let anyone hurt you. I need you to tell me the truth so I can find your family."

"They live underwater."

Hayjen blinked. "Underwater?" he questioned.

Her face jerked up and down in his hands. "Yes."

He barely kept the scowl from his face. Someone had been telling her old fish tales. "That's an interesting story. Thank you for telling me."

Mer beamed at him and pulled his hands from her face. "Are you hungry?"

"I'm always hungry."

"Come on, then."

She pulled him from the rail and to the galley, skipping along the deck waving and calling out hellos to the rough-looking pirates who all returned her waves and greetings with large smiles. Out of habit, Hayjen had searched the men for anything untoward.

Nothing.

Just affection.

He'd been on that damn Scythian ship too long. He was paranoid.

Hayjen forced his shoulders to loosen as he followed the little girl to the galley filled with the decadent smell of freshly baked bread. His eyes widened at how many people were packed into the space. Laughter, jokes, and smiles filled the room. Something loosened in his chest at the sound. It had been a long time since he had experienced this kind of camaraderie. Right in the middle of all of it was Captain Femi. She sniggered at something and punched her first mate in the arm before catching Hayjen's eye.

"Sleeping beauty awakes!" she hollered over the din.

Chuckles ripped through the group as her first mate stood and made his way towards Hayjen. "Pay no mind to her. They procured some type of tuna for dinner and she's overly excited about it." The man held out his arm. "We've not met officially. I'm Blair, first mate of the Sirenidae."

He clasped Blair's arm. "I'm Hayjen."

"Guardian of Mer."

"Yes."

Blair's severe face cracked into a soft smile. "She's a lovely little girl."

"She is indeed."

The first mate slapped him on the back and gestured to the serving line. "Fill up and eat, then we'll discuss whatever is plaguing you."

He watched as Blair wound around the group and slipped in next to the captain. She moved without looking at him, putting bread on his plate. The first mate plucked the bread from the plate and plopped his extra fish onto her plate. Each move was unconsciously coordinated, like they had done it a million times before. It was intimate in an understated way. If they weren't together, he'd ride a Leviathan.

Hayjen thanked the cook as he dished up his plate. He spun and scanned the room for the girls. They were huddled in the corner eating and watching the display of pirates like it was a play. Carefully, he navigated the throng of people, managing not to spill his plate. Beth held her hands up for his plate so he could sit without pulling his back. "Thank you."

She set his plate on the low table and winked. "It was nothing."

He blinked. Where had *that* come from? "How are you ladies this evening?"

A murmur of "good" sounded around him before they went back to watching the spectacle of pirates with curiosity. What he noticed though, was that each bowl that had been placed down on the table looked like it had been licked clean. They understood the value of food and what it was like to go without. He doubted any of them would leave leftovers anytime soon.

The pirates finished their food and eventually filtered out of the galley, the girls slipping out a couple at a time. Soft music filtered in from outside, jovial in its tune.

"Music?" Hayjen asked the few remaining women without addressing any one of them in particular.

"They play every night," Lera explained, unfolding from her pillow.

"Huh." The crew weren't what he expected when he thought of pirates. "Not all that pirate-like are they?"

Lera grinned at him. "Not what I imagined."

"Indeed." He smiled and glanced at Lilja. "Excuse me, I need to speak with the captain."

Her eyes darted to the captain and first mate who hadn't moved from their seats, and back to Mer pestering the cook. "I'll take Mer so you can speak with the captain."

"Thank you, Lera. I'd appreciate it."

"Let's listen to the music, Mer." Lera offered her hand.

The little girl shoved the rest of her bread in her pocket and skipped over to grab Lera's hand. "Let's go."

Hayjen watched with a bemused smile as Mer skipped out of the galley dragging Lera behind her.

"She's adventurous."

"Yes, she is." Hayjen commented before turning to the captain standing over him. His eyes roved up her long leather-clad legs and tapered waist, and paused when he met her eyes. The color was so different from anything he had ever seen. Exotic, and unearthly. Her brows raised in question at his stare. "Sorry," he mumbled. "Your eyes still intrigue me."

The deep chuckled that poured from her throat sounded way too sensual. "You and everyone else. My crew still stares at them sometimes and they've been with me for years."

He cocked his head, scanning her face. She couldn't be that old, maybe 24. "Years?"

"The sea has been my home all my life."

Ah. She had been raised on a ship. That made sense. "Was this your family's ship?"

"I inherited it, yes."

Smiling, he hefted himself from the low pillows and stared down at her. Her answers were answers, but vague. What was she hiding? "So where shall we speak?"

"In the study."

Hayjen blinked and looked over the captain's shoulder at Blair. He'd forgotten the first mate was even there. He stepped aside to let the captain and first mate lead the way. His nose twitched as he stepped into her study, citrus permeating the room in a clean, pleasant way. He moved to the side and sat in one of the chairs Captain Femi gestured to. Her first mate closed the door and moved to her side.

"What would you like to speak about?" she asked.

"Our deal, but I wanted to thank you again for your kindness to my people."

"It was nothing."

He ignored how his back pulled as he leaned forward, drawn to her citrus scent. "It's not nothing. We owe you our lives, but that being said, I wanted to make sure our original agreement was still in place."

"Yes. Your people will be returned to Aermia."

"Safely. To their families."

"Yes."

He sucked in a breath before asking a question that was plaguing him. "What do you expect in return?"

Captain Femi raised a brow. "Nothing."

Hayjen scoffed and sat back. "No one wants nothing. You've freed us, housed us, fed us, and are transporting us home. You and your crew have gone above and beyond what was needed. I would rather know what you expect from us sooner rather than later."

"We expect you to treat our crew with respect and help with the chores. That's it," Blair explained. "Other than that, you've no obligation or debt to us."

"Some pirates you are."

Captain Femi smiled, a twinkle in her eye. "We are a special brand of pirate."

"I can see that." Hayjen eyed the couple. "I have a few questions I would like answered."

"We will answer you to the best of our

knowledge."

"What did you want with that Scythian ship?" The couple traded glances. Interesting. "I was on that ship for months and was forced to work on it. I'm certain there were no treasures or cargo of interest for people like you. You're not so daft as to target just any random ship, and your taking over was well thought out and executed carefully. What were you after?"

"The Scythians stole something of great value to its owners. We were paid handsomely to retrieve it," Captain Femi readily replied.

"Did you find it?"

"No, we found you," Blair interjected.

"Was that a surprise?"

"No."

He froze, his mind spinning. "We're not the first slaves you've come across?" Silence. Hayjen blew out a breath. "How many?"

"Ships or slaves?" Captain Femi asked softly.

His fists clenched. "That many?" How long had Scythia been playing dead but secretly stealing their people?

Emotion rippled across Blair's face. "You're not the first or the last, but maybe one of the luckiest."

He stared at his clenched fists working through his feelings. He and the girls weren't a whim of a rogue Scythian ship. They were systematically abducting Aermian citizens, specifically women. His head snapped up. Why hadn't the crown taken action? "Why hasn't the king done something about it?"

"The Scythians are cautious. Nothing can be traced back to them. Also, there's limited communication between the two kingdoms."

He looked at the couple, flabbergasted. "But you have witnesses." He stabbed a finger at the door. "An entire crew of them."

A mocking chuckle rumbled out of Blair. "You really think the king is going to take the word of pirates?"

"The girls and I could go forward."

Captain Femi steepled her fingers and watched him over them. "Some have stepped forward in the past, but without proof nothing has come of it. Plus, Scythia has kept to their side of the wall for over two hundred years—to others, it seems impossible that they would steal people."

"You're telling me," he growled, "that those girls won't receive justice for what happened? That the Scythians will get away with what they're doing? Even if we were the only ones abducted, it's still wrong. How can the crown turn a blind eye?"

"That may be the case, but there's no proof. Something of this magnitude needs tangible evidence. It could start a war."

"It should," he retorted hotly.

"Do you remember nothing of the Nagalian Purge? The Scythians wiped out an entire race of people, not to mention their dragons. Would you be so quick to put Aermia in Scythia's sights?"

He swallowed hard. The Nagalian Purge was a blight no one would ever forget. In a matter of days, Scythia had coordinated an attack so brutal and swift that no one had survived. The Nagalian people were wiped from the world like they'd never existed. The other kingdoms had banded together and pushed Scythia behind their borders before building the Mort Wall to keep them exiled from the other kingdoms. He'd seen first-hand how dangerous they were. They were faster and stronger than they should have been. The image of Scythians flowing over the Mort Wall in waves gave him the chills. No one could survive that. "So what do we do?"

"You do nothing. You return to your home and help those girls settle back into their lives. You make a life for yourself."

Hayjen stared at the captain and first mate, a bit numb. How could he go back to the life he lived before? Nothing could erase the suffering he had experienced for months, or the knowledge that the Scythians would continue their nefarious activities. His eyes narrowed as a thought occurred to him. They said *you do nothing*, not *we do nothing*. "And what do *you* plan on doing?"

Blair's lips lifted into a sharp smile. "Pirating, of course."

Pirating, my ass, thought Hayjen. "Does said pirating involve looting more Scythian ships?" he needled.

The captain leaned forward, a glint in her exotic eyes. "We're pirates—nothing more. My crew and I risked our necks to help you when we had no obligation to—when most of our brethren would have left you to die or sold you to a new buyer. You and your girls are guests on my ship. What happens after we return you to Aermia is none of your concern."

That was fair. "I understand." He went to stand, but just as he did so, the captain's husky voice wrapped around him.

"We do have a few questions for you."

He slowly lowered himself back down into the chair and eyed the couple. "What can I help you with?"

"Did the Scythians ever speak of other shipments?"

"No." He shook his head. "They didn't speak much unless it was to torture someone."

The captain's face pinched at his words. "Was there a specific place where they were planning to drop you off?"

His brow wrinkled as he thought back to his time on the ship. "No. There's nothing." He paused, a spark of something coming forward. He vaguely remembered the warriors taking bets on if he would survive the trip to the caves. Hayjen scrubbed a hand down his face and traced the grains of the captain's desk with his finger. "After one of my beatings, the warriors took bets on if I would survive the journey to the caves of some sort." He lifted his eyes as the first mate swore viciously. "Does that mean something to you?"

Captain Femi glanced at her first mate, then at him. "Just that you're very fortunate we found you before you arrived at your destination."

His lips thinned at her vague response. It was like the woman didn't know how to give a straight answer.

"Thank you for your time. That's all we needed." Captain Femi stood and fluidly moved around her desk and held her hand out.

Hayjen stared at it for a beat before clasping it in his large hand. Her hands were so small and delicate in his, but they weren't the hands of a lady. She had callouses along her palm and fingers that spoke of hard work. The captain tugged her hand from his, making him blush like a besotted idiot. He had held her hand for longer than was appropriate. Hayjen pushed himself from the chair and nodded to both of them. "Good evening. I have a little one to put to bed." He shuffled to the door, pulled it open and slipped through, closing it behind him. He let out a little breath before moving forward. They hadn't given him all the answers he wanted, but he knew more now than he had going in. At least he had assured the girls safety, and that's what was most important. He would have plenty of time to analyze what he'd learned, but for tonight he was just going to enjoy the music with Mer.

Chapter Six

Lilja

She was relieved that the girls had settled in easily among her crew. Each day one of them showed progress. Sometimes, it was as simple as saying "thank you" during lunch. They all still had a haunted look in their eyes, but Lilja kept them busy enough that they couldn't dwell on their time on the Scythian ship. She counted that as a success.

Hayjen, their burly leader was a much harder nut to crack. His face was perpetually serious unless he was playing with Mer, when the smile on his face was suddenly radiant. He was a handsome man when serious, but he was jaw-dropping to look at when he smiled. His back healed quicker than expected, much to do with her seaweed concoction. As soon as he was able to stretch without tearing open his back, he moved to the girls' barracks.

That first night, she had crawled into bed thankful not to have to sleep on her window seat. Lilja had sighed when his musky, clean scent enveloped her before it dawned on her. She was sighing over a man. She practically leapt out of bed and yanked all the blankets off her bed. But even then, she could still smell him. With angry movements, she gathered up the blankets and stormed out of her room. Blair raised an eyebrow at her when she tossed the linens onto the deck with the demand that they be washed. Lilja gave him a rude gesture and stomped back to bed.

The next day she glared at the male interloper. How dare he smell so good! He never seemed to catch her glares or how she studiously avoided breathing too heavily around him, which was utterly ridiculous. She was a damn Sirenidae! One born to be alluring. Much to her delight she found he didn't understand teasing. Lilja made it her goal to shock him at least once a day. Her crass jokes and unusual clothing made him blush the most. The other girls caught on to what she was doing, and a few offered her suggestions—much to her surprise. It was nice to have women on the ship. She missed female companionship every now and again.

The days sped by and screeched to a halt when

they reached the coral beds. Colorful coral created a cage of sorts around some of the most breathtaking ocean life and seabeds. The only way to enter was to dive underwater and enter from a small archway the coral had created. Her people loved to visit, and each year they would make sure the arch was well-maintained so you could enter unharmed. The arch was also small enough that Leviathan could not enter. It was a safe place to play.

They weighed anchor, and her crew practically vibrated with joy. Lilja always made sure they stopped to take a swim. It was a part of her home and past that she could still enjoy—but not this time.

Lilja blew out a breath as her crew excitedly got ready for their swim, longing to get into the water with them. But even with her scarf, she couldn't take the chance of their guests seeing her gills. It wasn't safe.

It would be a death sentence. The stories of old painted gruesome pictures of her kind. Generation after generation were taught to fear and hate Sirenidae. Lilja had friends who'd been slaughtered out of fear and prejudice. She couldn't take the chance after knowing them for so little time.

Blair's hand slipped over hers as he gazed at the coral beds. "You'll be able to swim soon."

"I ache." Lilja touched her chest. "It physically

pains me not to swim with them. The ocean is calling to me."

"I know."

She gritted her teeth at the longing rolling through her.

"I have an idea."

Lilja tore her eyes from her sanctuary, meeting Blair's gaze. "What?"

"Mer's parents come for her tonight, correct?"

"Yes."

His eyes lit up. "Well, Mer will need someone to escort her."

Her heart soared for a moment as she thought about playing in the sea. But her enthusiasm was short-lived. At some point, they would have to drug Hayjen so they could return Mer to her family. He couldn't know the young girl was Sirenidae. She had to protect her people from the land kingdoms at all costs. Their secrecy was their strongest weapon. "The next week is going to be rough."

Blair nodded. "It's been peaceful the last couple weeks."

She smiled at her friend. "It's all the women."

His lips turned up. "They certainly improve our surroundings."

Her smile faded at the thought of how the girls would react to Mer's disappearance. "They may need to be held as well, but I don't want them drugged. It could damage their psyche more than it already is if we did that."

Her first mate's smile disappeared. "I don't want to lock them up after all they've suffered, but you're right—I doubt they will stand down."

Lilja turned and stared out at the waves. "Depths below, let's all hope we survive Hayjen's wrath."

"Aye, no good deed goes unpunished."

"Indeed," she added gravely.

Lilja's stomach knotted as Hayjen finished the food on his plate. Blair's hand landed on her leg, squeezing gently. She cast a sidelong glance at her friend.

"You were thumping," he said quietly between bites.

"Sorry," she grumbled, turning back to her own plate. Lilja pushed the food around on her plate, her ears straining to hear the conversation one table over.

"Time for bed, Mer."

"Awww...do I have to?"

"Yes, baby girl. It's time."

She just barely kept her eyes from watching the pair leave the galley.

"Calm down," Blair admonished softly.

She blew out a breath, angry with herself. She liked Hayjen, but returning the little girl and protecting her secret were more important. One by one, her crew and the girls filed out, leaving Blair and her alone.

"He's probably gone by now."

"I know."

Her first mate raised a brow at her tone.

Her lips thinned. Why was she feeling so guilty when she was doing the right thing?

"You know you have to do this."

"I know."

Blair straightened and wrapped an arm around her. "It's going to be okay. The next week will be filled with turmoil, but after that, the survivors will be gone and things can go back to normal."

Unexpected tears pricked her eyes. "I know," she sniffed. "I just...it's been a long time since I've felt at home, or had a measure of peace. Having the girls on board has been an unexpected blessing, and Mer...well, I will miss my niece."

"I've seen the change in you. You're a people person. They make you happy."

"Am I?" she wondered out loud. She didn't feel like she was a people person.

"More than myself. You seek others out. You don't

have to be liked, but you enjoy it."

"I don't think anyone likes to be disliked."

Blair's chuckle rumbled her shoulder. "You're right."

Lilja groaned, straightening and wiping her tears. "I don't have time for this." She forced a smile and pecked Blair on the cheek. "You'll make sure all the girls are tucked in?"

He watched her for a moment and nodded. "They'll all be in bed."

She sucked in a deep breath and stood from the pillows. "I'll get Mer." Lilja spun on her heel and swiftly strode from the room. She crossed the deck and moved into the girl's barracks. She waved at the women still awake and slipped in next to Hayjen's and Mer's hammocks. Hayjen was out cold. His mouth was wide open, deep breaths moving his chest. Mer popped her head up, grinning. Lilja knelt and smiled at the little girl. "Would you like to go for a swim?"

"Yes," Mer squealed.

Lilja held a finger up to her mouth. "Hush, we don't want to wake the others."

Mer slithered over the unconscious Hayjen, her eyes glittering with excitement.

She held out her hand for the little girl and took one last glance at Hayjen, guilt cramping her stomach. *Please forgive me*, she thought.

Lilja turned and began weaving through the swaying hammocks filled with sleeping girls. Lera lifted her head.

"I'm taking Mer for a swim. Is that alright?" Lilja asked. The petite woman smiled and closed her eyes. Lilja let out a breath and walked through the door with Mer skipping beside her. Mer dropped her hand and scrambled over to Blair leaning against the wall. She leapt into his arms, hugging him. A lump formed in Lilja's throat when Blair hugged the girl just as tightly and gazed over Mer's shoulder at her. He would have made a wonderful father. Their connection broke when Mer pulled back and began chattering excitedly.

"Lilja is taking me swimming! I might see a dolphin."

"Really? Now?"

"Uh huh!" She kicked her legs to get down.

Her first mate followed the silent prompting and placed Mer on the ground. Mer reached for Lilja and Blair's hands "Can we go now?"

The trio made their way to the open deck where her crew had made themselves scarce. They knew her secret, but they still respected her people's laws and secrecy. Two black fins sliced the water, alerting her to the arrival of Mer's parents. Lilja dropped to her knees and clasped the little girl's face. "Would you like to see your parents?"

Mer's lilac eyes rounded in her small face. "You found them?"

"They found you!"

The little girl jumped in place with a huge smile adorning her face. Lilja made sure to sear this memory in her mind. Mer ran for the edge of the ship and paused at the rail, "I forgot to say goodbye to Hayjen. I can't leave without saying goodbye."

"I'll make sure to tell him," Lilja whispered, caressing one of her niece's chubby cheeks.

Mer hugged her leg and looked up to Blair. "Can you throw me? My papa always does that."

"You don't want us to swim with you?"

"Nope, I like flying."

"I sure can, little one," Blair added.

Lilja looked down to the silent Sirenidae couple, their magenta eyes pinned to her, their pale skin glowing in the moonlight. "She's all yours, sister."

The couple clutched each other and tears filled their eyes when Blair hoisted Mer up.

"Mama! Papa! Watch this!"

Her first mate picked up Mer and then tossed her over the rail. The little girl squealed in delight as a loud voice bellowed, "NO!"

Lilja spun to find Hayjen horror-stricken. "No," he

cried, staring at the railing.

"Damn it," Blair hissed, moving quickly to intercept Hayjen.

Her sister needed to leave now. Mer's parents were cuddling the little girl, peppering her with kisses. Lilja jerked forward and waved, catching their attention. "It's not safe."

Lily peeked over Mer's head. "Thank you. I miss you."

She slumped against the railing, staring at the Sirenidae woman. "I miss you too," she called over the hollering.

"Love you," her sister's musical voice floated to her.

Tears blurred her eyes. She hadn't heard that voice in years. "I love you too, sis."

Mer blew her a kiss and dove into the water just as something huge smashed her into the railing. Her breath rushed out, and she tried to inhale but her lungs screamed.

"I'll kill you," Hayjen screamed next to her ear.

His weight lifted off her and she sunk to her hands and knees gasping for breath.

"How could you? She's just a little girl! What kind of monster are you?"

Lilja peered up at the out-of-control Hayjen fighting against Blair and Cook.

"You're a murderer." His face was purple. "You killed her. You killed her!" His scream cut off into ragged sobs of someone who had lost everything.

Blair and Cook dragged him to the stairs leading to the cells below deck.

She placed her forehead on the deck, still able to hear the muffled cries.

"Captain, do you need anything?" her deckhand's soft voice floated above her.

"No, thank you." She listened to his feet move away from her. Lilja knew she should get up, but the will to move wasn't there. She could still see her sister diving below without another glance backward, and Hayjen's panic-stricken face in her mind. There wasn't any way he would forgive her after this night.

Boots thudded across the deck in her direction and paused by her side. Large, careful hands plucked her from the deck and cradled her against a warm body.

"Oh, Lil."

So much was said in that brief statement. Blair was sorry she couldn't speak with her sister, sorry that she had to keep it from Mer that she was her aunt, sorry that Hayjen hated her—just sorry.

"I need to go to bed," she murmured against his sea-stained shirt. Blair tucked her underneath his arm and guided her towards her rooms. Once inside, Lilja sunk onto her window seat, staring out at the black waves hiding everything she cared about.

Her door clicked shut. "Do you want to talk about it?" Blair asked, sitting next to her.

Her eyes traced the swirling colors painted on the glass as thoughts whirled through her. "I miss them. I long to be with my family."

Blair's hand slipped into hers. He shared her pain. He knew what it was like to be separated from your people.

"After all this time," continued Lilja, "I thought the longing had faded away. But when I saw Lily's face, all I wanted to do was jump into the waves after her." A fat tear plopped onto her cheek, making her feel angry. "I hate that I've been punished for doing what is right." She turned to Blair. "Am I doing what's right?"

"I am thankful you didn't turn your back on the rest of the kingdoms like your family did. If you had, I would not be here with you. I would be stuck in that hell."

Lilja swallowed and closed her eyes. The decision to exile herself with those who dwelled upon the land had been easy. She had known it was the wrong decision to retreat to the sea when Scythians had attacked Nagali. Hiding didn't solve the Scythians' corruption or conquest for perfection. All it did was save her people's own skin. In deciding to help the other kingdoms, she had exiled herself from ever returning to the depths of her home. The claim was that she would be tainted by the world and endanger the others. The Sirenidae had faded from most people's minds and were now considered a myth. But Lilja was living proof that the Sirenidae were alive and well. Even as the pain of seeing her sister coursed through her, she knew she had made the right decision. If you had the power to prevent a crime, then it was your responsibility to do so.

She'd seen firsthand what the Scythians were doing. Lilja couldn't bear to leave the ignorant kingdoms on their own. She couldn't do much now other than steal back the slaves they captured, but one day she would make a stand against those beasts. Justice and vengeance would be served.

"You look as if you have the weight of the kingdoms on your shoulders."

"Don't we?" Lilja asked with a weak smile.

Blair studied her, his brown eyes keen. "We could always settle down."

Lilja slammed a hand against the window and stood. She ran her hands over her silvery white braid in agitation. "That's not what I meant. It's just—" She turned sharply and met Blair's eyes. "I am tired of waiting for the perfect time to strike Scythia, but we are just two people. We would need armies to defeat them, to destroy their labs. It feels hopeless."

Blair blew out a breath, dropping his eyes to her desk. "I feel the same way, but we must not be hasty. These things take time."

"I know." She truly did. "Then there's Hayjen."

Her friend's eyes lifted to hers. "He was very angry."

She rubbed her mouth, trying to figure out what to say. "I can still hear him screaming."

"He thinks we threw Mer to the Leviathan."

Her eyes widened.

"He didn't see your sister and her husband. All he saw was her being thrown overboard into the water. The Sirenidae's existence is still safe, but now he thinks we are murderers." Blair's voice was bland, betraying that he was upset over the ordeal. "I thought you drugged him, Lilja."

"I did. He shouldn't have woken until tomorrow morning."

"Well, something didn't work. Cook and I had to knock him out to get him contained."

"So he believes we murdered his adopted daughter?"

"Yes." Blair stared at her resolutely. "If he has the chance to kill you, he will."

Lilja let that settle for a moment. If she was in his position, she would feel the same way. "I can't say that I blame him."

"No," Blair added. "This week is going to be brutal."

"I can only imagine."

It was brutal.

Hayjen raged in the belly of the ship, bellowing himself hoarse.

The girls cried and cursed, then kept to themselves—speaking to no one but each other.

The whole ship filled with tension that set Lilja's teeth on edge.

When the Sanee port came into view, her frayed nerves settled a bit. They could rid themselves of the women and Hayjen, gather some supplies, and be on their way in a handful of days. Lilja adjusted her long flowing hair and dress as The Sirenidae glided into port. She waved to a few merchants smiling brightly. Most of them knew her as an eccentric lady merchant. When her ship shuddered to a stop, she swept from the rail towards the women's makeshift barracks. All eyes turned to her when she sauntered through the door. There were no welcomes or smiles, but rather blank faces and angry scowls.

It broke her heart that they'd lost the friendship and comradery they had built since she rescued them from the slaver ship. From the look in their eyes, she was no different than the monsters that hurt the girl, and that cut deep.

Lilja brushed it off as best she could and looked over the group. "We've arrived in Sanee." Emotions washed through the group; excitement, nervousness, apprehension, joy, resignation. "My first mate has arranged for transportation and some coins to help you start a new life or better your old one. You deserve happy, long lives."

"What of Mer? What did she deserve?" Lera growled.

"She deserved happiness, and a family."

"You're a monster."

Lilja schooled her face from betraying how much that hurt. "That may be so, but today this monster is returning you to your homes. I wish you every happiness and joy. May your lives be filled with love." With that parting remark, she swept from the room, saddened that she wouldn't see the group of girls again. One by one, her crew helped the girls disembark the ship. She watched with a sad heart as they hugged and cried when they left each other.

Once all the girls had left, there was just one to let loose. Lilja abandoned her perch and made her way down into the belly of the ship. The ship creaked as she halted in front of Hayjen's cell. He looked like a broken man, even worse than how they'd found him. It killed her that she'd done that. He'd survived so many things. She'd broken him.

"What do you want?" Hayjen lifted his head and locked eyes on her. Rage and hate blazed in his eyes as he lunged for her, slamming into the bars, his fingers barely skimming her dress. So close but not close enough to harm her. "I'll kill you."

She maintained a calm appearance even though her heart was pounding. It was the first time she'd visited him since returning Mer to her family. "I understand what you must be going through."

"You know nothing, murderer." His hands moved back to the bars. Hayjen shook them, a maniacal smile on his face. "When you release me, you better be prepared, captain—because there's nothing that will keep me from you."

"Indeed?" She arched a brow and cocked a hip. "I think there are many, but most importantly your sister."

Hayjen stilled. "What about my sister?" he growled.

"I have it on good authority that she's been taken in by another family, but I'm sure you would like to make sure of her welfare."

"How?"

"How do I know?" Lilja scoffed. "It's my business to deal in secrets. We've been in port less than an hour and I already know what is afoot in Sanee."

Hayjen just stared her with disgust. "Apparently you deal in death as well."

"Not everything is as it seems," she whispered.

"You're right," he rumbled. "I thought you were a decent person, but you're a bloodthirsty pirate without a conscience."

"How uninventive." She waved a hand. "I've been called worse."

"I'm sure it was appropriate."

Lilja glanced at the stairwell. She wasn't going to get anywhere. She wasn't sure what she had hoped to achieve by coming down those stairs, but it wasn't this.

"We've arrived in Sanee," she said in a monotone, not even bothering to turn back to face him. "My crew has arranged for transportation and coins for you to start a new life with your sister." She turned then to cast one last pitying look at the broken, angry man in her cell. "Good luck."

Her dress whispered around her legs as she ascended the stairs up to the deck. She sucked in a deep salty breath and blew it out.

"How was he?" Blair asked, stopping at her side.

"Angry, depressed, reckless."

"Can you blame him?"

"No, I cannot. But there's nothing we can do except get him off our ship."

Blair squeezed her shoulder and walked away.

Lilja's eyes slammed shut as yelling and fighting echoed from the belly of her ship, becoming louder. She turned and opened her eyes in time to watch her men drag Hayjen by his arms up the last of the stairs. Blood trickled from the corner of his mouth, causing her stomach to drop. She'd made a lifelong enemy.

He bared his teeth in a feral grin, teeth stained red. "Take a good look at my face, Femi. It will be the last thing you will ever see."

She kept her cool façade, just arching an eyebrow as he was pulled off her ship and thrown onto the dock below. "I doubt that, but you're welcome to try."

He pushed from his hands and knees, tipping his chin up to glare at her. "I don't try; I succeed."

The hair along the back of her neck rose. She didn't doubt him.

As she stared down at the man she'd broken, one thought was absolutely clear. He would come for her. It wasn't a matter of if, but of when.

Chapter Seven

Hayjen

Everything in his body screamed at him to storm the ship and wrap his hands around the pirate's slim neck. Rage, helplessness, and despair tumbled through him one after another like waves beating against the shore.

Mer.
Pain.
Rage.
Death.
Mer.
Helplessness.
Despair.
Rage.
Death.

He glared at the exotic captain and made a promise to Mer and himself that there would be justice. Her mouth stretched into an arrogant grin that said *do your worst.*

Hayjen was stunned for a moment.

When the captain smiled, she was breathtakingly beautiful. It was wrong that such beauty masked such evil and corruption, but her arrogance would be her downfall. He smiled inwardly; the young captain underestimated him. She wouldn't see him coming until it was too late.

Hayjen sketched a sarcastic bow and then forced his feet to move away from the ship. His neck prickled at all the eyes witnessing his departure. *Take a good look. You won't see me the second time.* He picked up his speed, anxious to see his sister and set his plan in motion. When his boots touched dirt, Hayjen's eyes grew damp.

He had made it home. Against all odds.

Fishers, merchants, and sailors scurried around him as he closed his eyes and reveled in the solid ground beneath his feet. When he opened them, Hayjen was a little lost. Where would his sister be? Even with their small savings, she wouldn't have been able to afford their home by herself with him gone. Where would she have gone? They didn't have many friends that could take on another mouth to feed. He shook his head and focused. He needed to check their old home first—if Gwen wasn't there, then he would speak to the neighbors. They were kind people, but nosey. They would have information about his sister.

Hayjen wove through the throng of people, putting the fishing district behind him. The tension in his shoulders released a bit as he passed familiar streets and homes. He swung around one last corner and spied his home. It was a rustic little shack made of dark stone with a well-kept wooden porch and two small windows, windows that were currently dark. The stairs complained as they always did as he stepped up to the door. His hand hesitated over the knob for a moment. Did he really want to see what was inside? He took a deep breath and entered. Light poured in through the doorway, illuminating the empty space. What had been such a cozy home was now an empty space with four stone walls and a fireplace.

"Gwen?" he called, knowing she wouldn't answer.

Nothing.

He moved further into the home, investigating both bedrooms. Both cold and empty. Hayjen turned and followed the tracks his boots made in the dust covered floor. He paused in the living room, despair clinging to him. He knew his sister wouldn't be here, yet some part of him hoped to walk through the door and spy Gwen sitting and reading in her favorite chair by the fireplace. He gazed in through the open doorway, dust floating in the air. He felt like his life had been erased.

Moving back outside, Hayjen took one last look at the place and closed the door to his life. He stared blankly at the homes around his. It still looked the same, but nothing was quite right. There were little changes here and there that left him feeling out of touch with the world. A ringing filled his ears, disorienting him.

"Haaaaay," a distorted voice called, but he couldn't even bring himself to search for the owner of the voice. All he could do was stare at the space in front of him as it undulated and changed colors. Nothing was right. He swayed as the world blurred around him. His sister, Mer, the Scythians. Nothing would be normal again.

"Hayjen!"

A sharp voice snapped him from whatever that was. He blinked a few times and noticed an old hand clutched his arm. Hayjen shook himself and squinted at the owner of the hand. A wrinkled old face with serious, grey eyes peered up at him.

Helva. An elderly neighbor.

"Well, sonny, I didn't expect you to show up here."

He stared.

Helva raised a brow. "You are Hayjen, aren't you? My old eyes aren't so good these days."

"It's me, old mother."

She smiled a crooked grin. "Stars above, I can't believe it! Come, come. Let's have some tea." She pulled on his arm with surprising strength and towed him towards her home. "Edwin!" she bellowed. "Edwin!"

"What are you shouting about this time, you old bat? Don't you know you'll irritate the whole neighborhood if you keep carrying on like that," Edwin shouted as he shuffled out the door with his cane. "I—" the elder man paused mid-rant when he caught sight of Hayjen. "Hayjen, my boy. Is that you?"

The little old man moved down the stairs and enveloped Hayjen in a hug. He still smelled the same, a bit like pine and smoke.

"I made it home," Hayjen choked out.

Edwin leaned back and scowled at his wife. "Why didn't you say Hayjen was home?"

Helva rolled her eyes. "You didn't give me a chance."

Edwin's eyes twinkled as he bent to give his wife a kiss on her weathered cheek. "Sorry, my love."

"Mmhmm..." she murmured with a smile and a twinkle in her eyes.

"Come inside, we'll feed ya, and you can tell us what has kept you all this time."

Hayjen froze. The couple had overwhelmed him such that for a moment Gwen had gone right out of his mind. Carefully, he pulled Helva's hand from his shoulder and kissed it. "Thank you for the invitation, but I need to find my sister. Do you know where she is?"

Edwin's open face turned wary. "Have you not been to see her?"

Hayjen dug deep for patience. "No, I have not. I don't know where she's been staying."

"She's with the Blackwells," Helva piped up.

"Blackwells?" His brows furrowed in confusion. "What in the blazes is she doing with the Blackwells?"

Helva patted him on the arm. "It's her tale to tell, but she's been well looked after. She visits us several times a week."

"That's nice," Hayjen remarked absently. He didn't know much of the Blackwells except that they were swordsmiths and the lady of the house had died years ago. "I need to go. Thank you for your information." He hugged the couple and sprinted towards the forge. His hairline had grown damp with sweat by the time the forge came into sight. Hayjen burst into the forge and gulped in a deep breath.

Gwen stood in the arms of a very tall man. Her eyes widened in shock.

No.

"Hayjen?" she whispered.

"I'm here," he panted as he opened up his arms.

With a cry, she flung herself out of the man's arms and slammed into him. Hayjen wrapped his arms around her, buried his face in her hair, and began to cry. He had held the pieces of himself together for so long that they crumbled into nothing when his sister began to sob in his arms.

"Where have you been?" she cried. "I thought you were dead. I searched for months."

"Shhhh…" he soothed through his own tears. "I'm here, I'm alright."

"I thought you had left me like papa and mum."

"Never," he choked out. "I'll never leave you."

Gwen pulled back, tears glistening in her hazel eyes. "Are you okay?" Her hands smoothed down his arms and then up to the tears on his cheeks.

Hayjen stared at his sister, his only family in the world. She kept him grounded. He had survived many things, because he had known he had to get back to her. "I'm okay, just happy I found you."

She clasped his hands. "Did you go by the old house?"

He nodded.

A smile bloomed across her face. "Helva and Edwin?"

Her smile pulled one from him. "Who else?"

A light-hearted laugh tumbled from her that eased all the tension in him. Gwen was safe. She was happy. He was home. It would be okay.

A large hand settled onto Gwen's shoulder. Hayjen's eyes narrowed as he met the moss- green eyes of Colm Blackwell. They crinkled as he smiled at Hayjen. Why was he smiling? Gwen cleared her throat, pulling his attention from the boy he faintly remembered. She blushed as she met Hayjen's gaze. His eyes jumped back to the smiling man and back again to his sister. *No.*

"Hayjen, you know Colm Blackwell," she paused, "my betrothed."

Hayjen opened his mouth and closed it and kept staring at the damn hand sitting on his sister's shoulder. *Betrothed?* "How?" he asked stupidly.

"The traditional way, you know. He asked, I said yes," Gwen joked.

His spine straightened. "Now is not the time to joke."

"Now's the perfect time. You came back from the dead."

He blew out a breath, trying to control the frustration and confusion that bubbled just beneath his surface. Nothing was right. Something was wrong with him. He should be happy for her, not feeling betrayed. "Could we speak outside?"

Gwen looked to Colm—*the interloper,* Hayjen thought.

He dropped a kiss on top of his sister's head. "Go spend time with your brother. I'll tell papa we have another guest."

"Thank you," Gwen whispered before taking his hand and leading him out of the forge.

They walked around the forge to where the forest came right up to the edge of the backyard. Hayjen pulled his hand from hers and stared at his sister. "What the bloody hell, Gwen? What is going on?"

"Let me explain."

"Please do."

"I've always liked Colm and his father."

"I can see that."

"When you disappeared, there weren't any who could take me in, so I needed a job. Colm's father Joseph had taken sick and they needed someone to help take care of the customers. I approached them and they gave me the job."

"Okay. What about the betrothal?"

Gwen scowled at him. "I haven't gotten that far. You need to calm down."

Hayjen took a deep breath. He did need to calm

down.

"Thank you. I began working in the forge and they paid me as well as they could. I traded some of my needlework for things I needed and lived as carefully as I could, but it wasn't enough to keep our home. I looked for other places to live, but no one would lease to a single woman of no means. I had nowhere to go."

His throat tightened. "Surely Helva and Edwin would have taken you in."

"They could barely take care of themselves. As it was, I was taking baskets of food to them so they didn't starve."

Gwen had such a generous heart. "Were you at least feeding yourself?"

"Yes."

He raised a brow. Hayjen knew his sister better than that. "You gave them your food."

She gave him a lopsided smile. "They took us in when mum and papa died. They had nothing and yet they took care of us until you found us a place to live. I would never let them go without when it was in my power to help. You would have done the same thing."

"I understand, Gwen. But at what cost?" He ran his hand through his hair. "You had to sell yourself. I'm so sorry."

His sister gasped, looking like he had slapped her.

"What *happened* to you? Surely you're not my brother. He would *never* say something like that to me."

He rubbed his eyes with his fists, angry that he had let something like that out of his mouth. "I'm sorry, sis. I didn't mean it."

"I know." She touched his arm and stared up into his eyes. "The Blackwells offered a home when I had none. Nothing improper happened despite the rumors floating around." Her face hardened. "My reputation was ruined the moment I stepped through their door."

"Did you accept a proposal to save your reputation?"

"No." Gwen shook her head. "The Blackwells have been very kind to me. They became close friends easily. Each day Joseph grew weaker, and the workload was left to Colm. He was struggling to keep up with the commissions, caring for his father, and feeding all of us. I began to cook and care for Joseph so Colm could work in the forge." His sister dropped her eyes. "They became my family."

Betrayal and hurt pooled in his gut. She was his only family and she'd found a new one while he fought his way back home. Hayjen knew he was being unreasonable, but he couldn't help it. He'd been replaced. He swallowed and forced a smile on his face. "I'm glad you were well taken care of."

Gwen nodded, not looking at him. "They have been good to me. After a time, Colm and I grew closer. One day, he asked for my hand. We were already friends," she chuckled, "and I was doing everything a wife would do anyway, so it was the right choice to make."

"Do you love him?" Hayjen asked. "If you don't, if you want out, I'll take you from this place right now."

She turned to him and touched his face, happiness shining in her eyes. "At first, I loved him like a friend, and we just fit. It was like breathing. But over time friendship grew into something so much more, something impossibly grand and wondrous."

The awe in her voice convinced him. Gwen didn't beat around the bush. She knew people and knew her own mind. She'd always had good judgment. If she loved Colm, he was a good man. "He sounds like a man mum and papa would have approved of," he said gruffly.

"I think so, but I would have your approval." Gwen smiled. "I mean—you did raise me."

His throat tightened. Carefully, he pulled Gwen towards him and kissed her forehead. "Well, I'll have to get to know him, but from your assessment, he sounds like someone I will become good friends with."

"I hope so."

Gwen hugged him tightly as he stared over her head at the forest. His sister was betrothed. Soon she would belong to another man, have a family of her own. Hayjen couldn't let go of what had happened to Mer. He closed his eyes as the pain of losing the little girl washed over him. He didn't know what would happen when he attacked the captain but now he didn't have to worry. Gwen would be taken care of.

"What happened to you?"

"It's a long story that will no doubt keep you from sleep."

"That awful?" she squeaked, horror in her voice.

Hayjen pulled back, chucking her on the chin. "It's a story for tomorrow. Tonight, we celebrate our new family and returning to those we love."

Her lips thinned. "You can't sweep this under the rug. I will keep asking."

A true smile adorned his face as he steered his sister back towards the forge. She was like a bloodhound when it came to something she wanted. At least that hadn't changed. "That I don't doubt."

"Come meet our family."

Family.

Mer had been his family.

Now she was gone. How long would this one last?

Chapter Eight

Hayjen

He wanted to hate Colm on principle, but the man was a saint. He was soft-spoken with a wicked sense of humor. Hayjen studied the couple through the doorway as they washed dishes that night after supper. Gwen didn't see the adoration in Colm's eyes while she scrubbed the dishes, but he could. The man was completely in love with her. He smiled as Colm bumped Gwen with his shoulder and she splashed him, causing them both to break out in a fit of giggles.

"They're well matched, I think," commented Joseph, the senior Blackwell.

Hayjen peered at the older man. He was pale and sickly, shivering even though he was right next to the fire. The old man looked at him through tired eyes.

"He'll take good care of Gwen. I've taught him to treat women with respect, tenderness, love. Gwen is precious to us both. We're lucky to have her in our lives."

"She brings warmth and light wherever she goes. You're right on that account."

"Gwen is a blessing. I am overjoyed to welcome her into our family, and you as well even if you leave."

He straightened, staring at Joseph. "What makes you say that?"

The old man shook his head, wearing a grim smile. "When my wife died, I was a shell of a man, then I grew angry and went looking for someone to blame." Joseph met his eyes. "You've got darkness in your soul—anger, hate. I don't know what happened to you, but you're looking to deal out some blame."

"That's very astute for one who's only known me for half a day."

A harsh laugh rumbled in the senior Blackwell's chest. "A man drowning in nightmares and vengeance is easy to spot." He paused then continued. "May I offer you a piece of advice I wished someone would have shared with me?"

"Share away."

"Vengeance does not bring peace." Joseph's emerald green eyes pierced him. "You think that avenging whatever plagues you will make the pain, the hurt, the guilt go away—but it doesn't. It multiplies or leaves you completely empty and numb. It's not a good way to live and it takes many years to claw yourself out of a grave you've dug for yourself."

Joseph Blackwell's words reverberated inside him. Could he let the hurt, guilt, and pain go? The rage that burned beneath the surface said no. Hayjen clasped his hand loosely between his knees and scrutinized the old man. "And if this person deserves justice? If I can't let go?"

"Be ready to accept the consequences of your actions," he said simply.

Hayjen turned to watch his sister and her betrothed tease each other and laugh.

"It's good to hear her laugh so freely," said Joseph. "It was a scarce sound when she first started working for us."

He turned back to Joseph rocking by the fire.

"She hunted for you for weeks when you didn't turn up from fishing. When she lost your home, she went back every day for months hoping to find you there. Each time she came back empty-handed about killed her. Unbeknownst to Gwen, Colm would search the fishing district for information about you each night. He just wanted her to be happy."

His heart warmed at that. Hayjen turned back to the couple as they entered the room hand in hand. Gwen kissed Joseph's cheek before sitting on the rug in front of the fire, uncharacteristically serious.

"Where have you been?"

Hayjen sucked in a breath and clenched his hands. "Until a month ago, I was on a Scythian slave ship."

Silence.

Everyone was frozen, staring at him in shock.

"A Scythian ship?" Colm finally asked.

"A Scythian ship."

"How is that possible?" Joseph questioned. "They haven't been in contact with Aermia since the Nagalian purge."

"The other slaves and I were kidnapped. We thought we were the first, but we received some information that said otherwise."

"What did they want?"

"With me? Hard labor is my guess. With all the women? I can only imagine. There were only four male slaves when I was captured. By the end of the week, I was the only male left alive." He paused, trying to sort through the nightmares and stick to the basics. "I wouldn't wish them on my worst enemy."

"Did they hurt you?" His sister's voice broke.

"Sis, you don't need to know."

She shook her head, brown curls whipping around. "No, I need to know."

Colm squeezed her hand. "My love, maybe it's painful to speak about."

Gwen's eyes widened. "I'm sorry, I didn't mean anything by it. I just—"

He understood. If Gwen had disappeared, he would have wanted to know, too. He heaved himself up, turned his back to the room and hauled his shirt over his head. Curses and a sob sounded behind him. A finger touched his back and jerked away.

"Does it hurt?" Gwen choked out.

"Not now, sis."

She traced one. "So many, Hay. So many. How did you survive?"

Hayjen craned his neck and caught his sister's eye. "Determination and seaweed."

"Now's not the time for jokes," she scolded.

"Now is always the time for jokes," he commented while shrugging on his shirt. "You never know when you'll be able to joke again." He spun and hugged Gwen, knowing she needed it after what she had just witnessed. His back was an ugly thing to behold. She stepped back and stared at his wrists. He lifted them and twisted them back and forth. "Cuffs."

Gwen rushed to the fire and vomited. Colm rushed towards her and stopped when she held a hand up. "I just need a minute." She heaved several more times before wiping the back of her hand across her mouth. "How did you escape those animals?"

Now it was his turn to feel sick. "Pirates."

"Pirates?" Joseph demanded. "Stars above—this tale just gets wilder and wilder. It's a miracle you escaped with your life!"

"Father," Colm chastised. "Show some empathy."

Joseph met his eyes with an apologetic look. "I let my mouth get the best of me. Forgive me."

"Nothing to forgive. If I heard my tale from someone else, I would hardly believe it."

"Did—did the other slaves escape as well?"

Lilac eyes. A sweet giggle.

Bile burned the back of his throat. He wouldn't share what happened to Mer with anyone. No one deserved to have those images in their minds for the rest of their lives. "Most, but not all."

"I am so sorry, brother."

He shrugged. "There's nothing to do but move on now."

All three of them looked at him like he was insane.

"You should report it to the crown. Scythians attacking Aermian citizens is something they should know about," Colm remarked.

"There's no proof."

"You're living proof, you daft boy," Joseph added.

"Others have gone forward, but to no avail. No one wants war with Scythia."

"So we keep letting them steal people?" Gwen snarled.

"I don't like it any more than you do. But what would you have me do?"

"I don't know," she huffed, frustrated tears in her eyes.

"I know your frustration, sis. I know. I feel it every time I look in the mirror or when a nightmare wakes me in the night."

Gwen blinked and visually pulled herself together. "I'm sorry, I am feeling so much right now." She stared at the rug for a moment before meeting his eyes. "We don't have to figure out anything tonight. It will keep to the morning as mum used to say. You're probably exhausted. Would you like to go to bed?"

He was weary to his bones and a bed sounded wonderful. "I could sleep."

His sister's trembling lips morphed into a full blown smile that crinkled the corners of her eyes. That had been their papa's favorite saying when their mum used to call for him to come to bed.

"It's good to have you home."

"It's good to be home."

It didn't feel like home anymore.

Things were the same, but so different. Gwen had grown up while he was gone. She was still her bubbly self, but she worked hard and took on more responsibilities. When Joseph had become sick, Colm had taken over the work in the forge—he was a little behind on a few commissions, so over the following weeks, Hayjen pitched in doing what he could.

One night, after a particularly long day of stoking the fires and cleaning swords, his thoughts wandered towards his nightly activities. Every night he had snuck out and down to the docks, hoping for an opportunity to sneak aboard the ship. Much to his irritation, there never was a good time. The captain was always surrounded by people. He'd inquired about her and practically destroyed a pub when he heard all the praise sung about her. Captain Femi had all the merchants eating out of the palm of her hand. It sickened him to think that such beauty held such corruption.

He pulled at some grass, venting some of his frustration. To make things worse, he'd received news that the ship was to sail in the morning. He had only this evening to make his plan work, only one opportunity.

"Still glowering at the forest? What did it ever do to you?"

Hayjen tilted his head up and smiled at Gwen as she plopped down into the grass next to him. She tipped her head back, eyes closed with a smile on her face. Her love for the sun hadn't changed in the least.

"Enjoying the peace and quiet," he said.

"Now *that* I believe." She cracked open one eye. "I'm happy you're home."

"So am I." He swallowed hard and tried to think of something else to say. When he was on the Scythian ship, he'd imagined having conversations with her—but now that she was within arm's reach, he didn't know what to say. So he said nothing.

"You know you can talk to me, right?"

"I know."

"Is it," a pause, "a woman?"

"What?" he asked sharply.

Gwen opened both eyes and stared at him shrewdly. "You've disappeared each night, only to return in the early morning." Her mouth turned downward. "Mum taught you better."

"It's not a woman."

"If it's not a woman, then where are you going?"

"Out."

Her eyes narrowed. "That's not an answer."

"Sis, it's all you need to know."

"Why?"

"For your own protection."

Her hand settled atop his. "Who is protecting *you?*"

The concern in her voice touched him. "I am alright."

"You're the furthest thing from alright." Hayjen stiffened, meeting her serious eyes. "You carry darkness around with you like it's your own personal cloak. Your smiles are forced and there's no light shining from your eyes."

He dropped his gaze to the grass, hating how much she really saw. "Sometimes the light is snuffed out."

"No one has that power over us unless we allow it."

"What do you know of it?" he retorted.

"Enough to know that you're in pain. Let me in, Hayjen. I can help."

"You can't change the past." No matter how much he longed to.

"No you can't, but you can come to terms with it. Speak and I will listen."

Hayjen swallowed and let one word roll off his tongue. "Mer."

"Mer," Gwen repeated. "What does it mean?"

"Glittering Sea."

"Pretty."

A smile bloomed across his face. "She was. Mer's

hair was so blond it was almost white, and she had the loveliest lilac eyes. Her giggle was as infectious as her sass." His smile melted when he looked at Gwen. "The Scythians enjoyed tormenting her and I couldn't bear to see a child treated that way."

His sister gasped. "A child?"

"Yes," he choked out. "She latched onto me and I to her. I made sure she was fed, her wounds bandaged. I tucked her in at night and said a prayer with her. It was like she was—"

"Yours," Gwen breathed.

"I promised her that I would get us off the ship and that I would look for her parents. If I didn't find them, I planned on keeping her."

His sister blew out a breath before asking, "What happened to her?"

Mer's happy face flew through his mind as she waved to him before disappearing over the side of the ship when black fins gleamed. Bile crept up his throat. He wouldn't wish his nightmares on anyone. "She was murdered."

"Stars above, Hayjen. Did you alert the authorities?"

He barked out a harsh laugh. "Do you really think they care? Like they care about Scythians torturing their people? No one cares but me. Don't let it be said that justice doesn't prevail."

Gwen stilled. "What do you mean?"

"That filth won't get away with what they did. They will come to a violent end as terrible as their souls."

"That's not justice, that's revenge."

"In this case, it's the same."

"No." His sister shook her head, her braid whipping through the air. "It's not. You taught me that as a child. You're seeking revenge."

Hayjen glared at his sister. "Does she not deserve justice?"

"Yes, but not by your hand."

"I won't let them get away with this."

"*You* won't let them get away with this? Who appointed you judge, jury, and executioner?"

"You don't understand what it is like to lose someone."

"How can you say that to me? I lost mum and papa just like you did, not to mention I lost you for months. I thought you were dead!"

"I did die. The Hayjen you knew died on that ship along with a little girl. I will wipe them from this world so they can't hurt another."

"It's murder."

He glared at Gwen and she glared right back, rising onto her knees.

"Your thinking isn't clear," she said.

He scoffed. "It's the clearest it's been in a long time. They need to be put down."

"Like animals? Are you even hearing yourself? They're still human, despite their wrong actions. Human beings."

"If they act like animals, they should be treated like animals!" he bellowed, jumping to his feet.

"It's murder!" Gwen yelled back, standing up, her chest heaving.

Colm poked his head out of the forge, looking concerned. "Is everything okay?"

Gwen broke their stare off, peeking over her shoulder at her betrothed. "We're alright. We're just talking."

The swordsmith glanced between them before disappearing into the forge. Gwen turned back to him, sadness in her eyes. "Have you thought of the cost? Truly? If you go down this path, then you will become the thing you hate. You will become just like them."

Hayjen slammed his eyes closed like it would keep her words from taking root. Mer deserved justice and so did he. "I need this," he whispered and opened his eyes. "Gwen, I need this."

Her face crumpled as tears filled her eyes. "You don't—you just can't see that." One sob escaped her, breaking what was left of his heart. "You were right when you said my brother died on that ship. I don't know who you are. And I can't save you from yourself." She closed the distance between them and grabbed his hand. "I love you. You're my brother. You've been my only family for so long. But if you choose this path, you can't be part of my life anymore."

He stiffened, his eyes darting between her hazel ones. "Are you threatening me?" he choked out, everything going numb.

She shook her head violently. "No, just stating the truth." Gwen pulled his hand to her flat belly. "I have to protect my own."

The numbness burned away at her implication. "Are you pregnant?" he hissed. Hayjen crooked a finger under her chin so he could look into her eyes. "Gwen, are you pregnant?"

"Yes."

Hayjen's eyes dropped to her belly. His sister would have a child. His unmarried sister. "I'm going to kill him," he growled, moving to go around her. His sister latched onto his arm. His angry eyes met her tear-filled ones.

"We're married."

For the second time that day, he went numb. She turned to look at him, guilt written on her face.

"I didn't want to overwhelm you. We had a simple

ceremony. Colm and I planned on having a big one if," she paused, "if you came home."

His lips moved not of his own accord. "It's wrong to lie even if it's to spare another's feelings."

"I know, brother, you taught me that. I'm sorry for not being honest."

His sister was going to be a mother. "Well, Colm didn't waste any time."

Gwen blushed then scowled. "I've always wanted a family."

She always had. It had been his dream too, at one time. Hayjen dropped to his knees and stared at Gwen's skirt like he could see the baby.

"There's nothing there." She smoothed her skirts so he could see her belly.

Carefully, he touched her belly and smiled. "Hello there, baby girl. I'm your uncle Hayjen."

"How do you know it's a girl?"

"Because you deserve to have one as wily as you were."

Gwen chuckled and sunk down to her knees. Her smile morphed into something much more serious as she clasped his face. "I want you to be part of our lives, but you need to decide what is most important."

"My decision was made the moment you told me you were pregnant."

Her sunny smile broke out on her face. "Thank God." Gwen gestured to her face and more tears poured down. "Damn body. All I do is cry."

He kissed her forehead and helped her to her feet. "Mum did the same thing with you."

"Really?" she asked.

"Truly. As a little boy, I didn't know what I'd done wrong. Papa had to explain to me that it wasn't my fault."

"I wish they were here."

"Me, too."

"You hungry?"

"Always."

Gwen led him inside and he felt a twinge of guilt at the happy smile adorning his sister's face. He'd told her the truth—his decision had been made the moment he found out she was pregnant. It just wasn't the decision she hoped for. Hayjen was more determined than ever to make sure no one could hurt his family.

Time to hunt.

Chapter Nine

Lilja

"You sure you won't come with us, Captain?"

She smiled at her rambunctious crew, shaking her head. "Do you remember the last time we descended on Sanee? Chaos and mayhem was the result."

"You just want to finish your book!" James shouted.

Lilja chuckled; her men knew her well. "That may be the case, but it doesn't make the former any less true."

"We didn't cause that much mischief."

"Tell that to the pub owner."

James shrugged a shoulder and charged forward down the dock. "To the ale we go!" he shouted.

She watched them joke and make a spectacle of themselves as they moved further away. "Hams. I have a crew made up of hams."

"The perfect fit, I must say."

Lilja stiffened then relaxed. "Damn it, Blair. Don't sneak up on me."

Blair leaned against the railing, his dark eyes glittering with mirth. "Don't be so obtuse. Then I wouldn't be able to sneak up on you."

"You and your warrior sneaking skills, useless," she muttered under her breath.

"Increased hearing as well, Lil."

She smiled sweetly. "Didn't forget."

His eyes narrowed and a sly smile crept across his face. Lilja stared at him with wide eyes. That look never boded well. "I am just going to go read." She began backing away and paused when his body stilled. "No!" she shouted as she spun to sprint towards her study.

Three steps. She only made it three steps before a large arm wrapped around her middle and the other was tickling her neck. "Stop!" she screeched in between bouts of giggles.

"Not until you admit that my skills are far superior and that you couldn't survive without me!"

"Never!" she growled between teeth.

"Okay then, Captain."

The tickling intensified so much that she couldn't breathe. "I give," she wheezed. "I give. Your skills on land are far superior to mine and I couldn't survive without you."

"Not quite right."

"You couldn't beat me in a swimming race and you know it."

Blair paused in his tickling. "I will concede that."

He set her down and Lilja straightened her clothes, scowling at him while he grinned. "No more of that."

"I can't help when the fancy to tickle you strikes."

"Sure you can. It's called keeping your hands to yourself."

"Where's the fun in that, Lil?"

Lilja smiled at his good-natured ribbing. It wasn't often that Blair was playful. When he was, she treasured every moment. "What are you doing this evening?"

"Fishing, lounging around."

"Fishing?" she scoffed. "When is the last time you fished for fun."

"My point exactly."

"Mmhmm…well I am going to finish my new book, so don't interrupt me. Then, I may go for a swim."

His face grew serious. "This close to other people?"

"I'll be careful. When I get back, most of them will be so deep in their cups that if they managed to spot me, they would doubt what they saw."

"Just keep your senses."

"Always do."

She waved and sauntered into her room, excited at the prospect of an evening to herself. Grabbing her snack off her desk, she moved to the nest of pillows and blankets in her window seat. With a grateful sigh, she sunk into the nest and squirmed until she got comfortable. Time to find out if the maiden found her true love.

What an ending!

Lilja blinked and rubbed her eyes. She glanced around the room, squinting. No wonder it was hard to see the words. Almost all the light had faded from the room. She laid her book down and stretched as she stood. A happy groan escaped her. Why did stretching feel so good? She dropped her arms, scanned the room and spotted her seal skin.

She marched toward it and snagged it off the rung. She couldn't wait to go for a swim. The seal skin suit made it so easy to glide through the water with speed. Lilja slipped on the one piece suit created for speed and wrapped a robe around herself. She snuck out of the room and out to the railing. Quickly, she surveyed the area. No one was around. She threw her robe over a barrel and climbed over the railing. Lilja sucked in one last breath before pushing off the side of the ship and into a dive.

Her skin tingled all over as the sea welcomed her back. She sucked in a breath and grimaced in pain as the air was shoved out of her lungs and her gills opened. The transition wasn't painless, but it was manageable. Lilja allowed herself to sink to the ocean floor, sand cushioning her knees. She opened her eyes and pushed the tendrils of her hair out of her face. There was nothing like swimming in the sea. Life teemed everywhere. Fish, crustaceans, corals, and sea stars decorated that land she called home.

Peace engulfed her, causing her to lie back and float. She soaked in the murmur of the sea. The quiet melody it was always singing. Little fish darted in, tempting her to give in and join their game of tag. Lilja swatted at them playfully and enjoyed her peace. When the little inhabitants of the sea went silent, she smiled. She sat up—her hair floating around her—and smiled at the dark creatures waiting for her silently.

The Leviathan.

She pushed from the sand and glided towards the beasts feared by many. She stopped before the alpha and hummed a little tune. All the Leviathan hummed in excitement. They loved to race. Lilja held her hand out in offering. The immense beast slid forward and bumped her hand, its black eyes never leaving her. She smiled and darted below her new race partner, gaining a head. Her muscles burned as she swam as hard as she could. A series of happy hums vibrated through the air. The race was on—it wouldn't be long before they passed her.

Sure enough, within moments the first of the dark shining beasts whipped above her and moved ahead. Dark shapes surrounded her, gliding in and out in patterns that astounded her in their beauty. Breathing out, she paused and continued to glide through the water. The alpha paused, noticing her slowing, and swam back to circle her. She was out of shape. No beast or man could outswim a Leviathan but she used to be able to keep up for a time.

She smiled when a young one bumped her with its nose and rubbed against her side. A sound like a purr rumbled out of the youngling when she scratched behind its dorsal fin. Lilja grinned as, one by one, each Leviathan of the pod moved in to receive its own massage. Last was the alpha—he circled her and rubbed against her finally. When she scratched him, the purr almost startled her in its loudness. Carefully, she ran her hand along his fin and floated above. She hummed her race song, hoping he would allow her to ride with him.

Without warning he jerked forward, startling a squeak out of her. He stopped at the sound and twisted back to nuzzle her leg. Lilja smoothed a hand down his side, letting him know it was okay—she was just surprised. The beast straightened and burst forward again, but this time she was prepared. She grinned as he raced against the rest of the pod, weaving in and out of his brethren, trying to impress her.

When they arrived at the coastal shelf, Lilja let go of his fin and swam around him. Again, she held her hand out respecting his choice to say farewell. He bypassed her hand and bumped her in the face. Honored and surprised, she wrapped her arms around his snout, avoiding the huge sharp teeth, and kissed his slick skin. "Thank you for the honor," she hummed. Lilja waved to the pod as they faded back into the darkness and slowly swam towards the harbor where the ships bobbed.

She stopped to flip a crab over and smiled as it scuttled away. The little crustacean would live another day. Satisfied with her swim, she moved towards the moonlight dancing on the water. Breaking through the surface, Lilja sucked in a breath. Her gills closed, forcing the water out of her lungs. She coughed, sputtering up sea water until her lungs were finally able to suck in great lungfuls of night air. She scanned the area before climbing up the rope ladder, which hung over the railing. Speedily, she reached the railing and hauled herself over. Lilja threw her robe over her seal skin and spun, moving towards her room.

The Lure would be strong, so she needed to get to her room. Something slammed into her back, crashing her into the hallway wall.

"Gods, you smell good," Blair growled, pressing his nose against her neck.

Hell.

Lilja closed her eyes and took a deep breath. "Blair, you need to think about what you are doing."

"What?" he asked, sounding dazed as his hands caressed her waist and his nose skimmed her jaw.

She gritted her teeth. "You are reacting to my smell. It's science, Blair. Pheromones. The sea water activated it. This isn't your choice. It's my protection. You are supposed to want me. It's who I am. It's just the Lure." His hands clenched on her waist then moved to the wall on either side of her, his face never leaving her neck.

"Damn it," he mumbled against her skin. "YOU. JUST. SMELL. SO. GOOD."

"I know, it's just the Lure. Once my scent leaves

you, your senses will come back. You need to step away."

Blair pressed his face further into her neck. "I'm sorry, Lil."

"Nothing to be sorry about, it's not your fault."

He nodded and then jerked himself from her and stumbled down the hall.

Lilja pushed off the wall, watching him stagger away. "Sorry."

"Damn sirens," he mumbled, shaking himself. "I'll be back in a couple of hours."

She tightened her robe and slunk into her room, closing the door. Stupid Lure. It turned men stupid around her. Lilja began to shrug off the robe sticking to her skin when something pricked her gill. Something suspiciously sharp and short, like a dagger.

"You will answer for what you've done."

Hayjen.

Nothing like ending your evening at knife point.

Lilja breathed shallowly so as not to provoke the man behind her into doing something they would both regret. "Calm down, Hayjen."

"Don't tell me to calm down, murderer."

She winced as her neck stung and she felt blood trickle down onto her collarbone. "Okay." Her eyes flitted to her desk where she had daggers stashed. If she could move him in that direction, she might be able to defend herself and knock him out. A tendril of fear snaked through her at the plan forming in her mind. Maybe if she went limp she could use her dead weight to unbalance him and get away. But she also ran the risk of being cut.

"Stars above," Hayjen muttered, pulling her back against his broad muscled chest. "What is that bloody smell?"

Lilja blinked. The Lure. Either the Lure would work in her favor—distracting him enough that she could escape—or it would anger him enough that his lust would turn to something sinister. His nose pressed behind her ear and his hand tightened.

"What is that?" he demanded, his voice tight. "It's like chocolate, citrus, and sin."

She squeezed her eyes closed and tapped into her sultry side. "What do you think it is?" She lifted a hand and ran it along the fingers gripping the dagger. "My body is calling to you." His voice hitched. Carefully, she drew a pattern on the forearm wrapped around her body. "Can't you feel it?"

"I don't know what you are talking about," Hayjen panted even as he pulled her closer, molding her to himself. "What is happening?" he whispered.

"Biology."

A hot tongue glided up her neck causing her

breath to stutter out in shock. He paused then jerked away, pulling her wet hair from her neck. "What the hell?" The arm around her body released her and touched one of her gills. "What in the hell is that?"

Lilja seized the moment of his distraction and wrenched the dagger far enough from her neck that she was able to slither out of his arms. Her hand stung from the cut, but she barely felt it as she lunged for her desk. Hayjen crashed into her, causing her to hit her head on the corner of her desk. Stars dotted her vision and her stomach rolled. Blindly, she kicked out and was satisfied when she felt her foot connect and a curse exploded out of Hayjen. She crawled to her knees, the world spinning around her. She needed to secure a dagger. He wasn't in his right mind. A hand landed on her hips and flipped her over. Lilja grunted and lashed out, hitting whatever she could. In a quick maneuver, her hands were pinned beneath knees as Hayjen sat on her hips. No matter how she bucked, the giant man didn't move.

"Stop moving," he growled.

"So you can kill me? I don't think so!" she hissed, the pain in her head so bad that tears dripped from the corners of her eyes.

"I said stop it." Cold metal touched her collarbone.

She stilled. The dagger danced along her skin, pushing her hair from her neck, and paused on her gills. Lilja's eyes slammed shut. By seeing her gills, he basically signed his own death warrant. Blair would never let him escape with her secret. "Don't," she pleaded.

"What are you?" Lilja felt him lean forward to study them. "What are these?"

"Just forget what you saw and leave."

"No, I want answers."

"I don't have any."

"Lies. Stop lying to me."

The darkness in his voice made the hair on her arms stand. She swallowed and uttered something she rarely admitted out loud. "They're gills."

Silence reigned in the room except for their harsh breathing. "You can breathe underwater?" he questioned.

She went to nod, but froze when the nausea overwhelmed her. "Yes."

Hayjen stiffened. "The dreams are real," he murmured. "Look at me."

Lilja squinted through her pain and met his untrusting eyes.

"Did you save me from the Leviathan?"

Staring back, she didn't blink. "Yes."

Hayjen's mouth pinched and the skin around his eyes tightened. "Why?"

"Because it was the right thing to do."

"Damn it." He pulled the dagger from her neck and slammed it into the floor. "Then why Mer?" he cried. "Why? She was only a little girl!"

"Hayjen."

"Why her? Why not me?"

"Hayjen."

"What?" he yelled, glaring down at her.

"Look at me."

His eyes filled with confusion. "I *am* looking at you."

"No," she said softly. "Look at me. Who do I remind you of?"

"No one. You're too unique to look like anyone I know."

"You're looking but not seeing. Think of possibilities. Who looks similar to me?"

Hayjen's eyes scrutinized her face. He paused when his eyes met hers. They just stared at each other until suspicion, recognition, and shock flitted through his gaze. "Mer."

Relief shot through her bones. The guilt of keeping the truth from him had weighed her down more than she'd realized.

"You're lying," he said.

"Why would I lie? Think, Hayjen. Doesn't it make sense?"

He cursed and looked out the window, his gaze

darting back to her eyes, face and hair—then to the window. "Mer?" he asked with so much longing and pain that it nearly killed her.

"Alive."

His breath rushed out of him, his eyes glazing over. "How?"

"Leviathan respect us."

"How can I believe you?" He shook her a little bit, causing blackness to encroach on her vision.

"The proof's in front of you," she gritted out. "You're alive and so am I."

"I want to see her."

"I don't know if you can, but I will try."

"Trying isn't good enough. I need to see her with my own eyes."

Frustration built in her. "There are laws."

"What are you talking about? What damn laws?"

"Sirenidae laws!"

Hayjen's eyes widened. "You are spouting nonsense."

"No, I'm not."

"The Sirenidae aren't real."

"Says who?" she challenged, feeling sick.

"History."

"Well, history isn't always correct. You felt the Lure."

He jerked back and scrambled off her. "You

controlled that?" he yelled.

Lilja grabbed her head, pain exploding as she tried to sit up. "No, I can't control it." She blinked at Hayjen as he blurred into three people. "I'm sorry," she whispered before everything went black.

Chapter Ten

Hayjen

Her eyes rolled back and she crashed to the floor. The loud crack had him back at her side in no time. "Lilja?" Nothing. Hayjen leaned forward and scanned her face, his stomach dropping. He was so angry that he hadn't noticed how badly she was bleeding. He grabbed her by the shoulders and shook her a bit. Still nothing. Damn. He quickly ripped a section of her robe off and wrapped the wound. When he pulled his hands back they were covered in blood. He blinked. She was bleeding on the back of her head, too? What should he do? He shuddered again at the sight of the strange lines on her neck. She wasn't human, but that didn't mean she shouldn't be treated with humanity. She needed a healer. But if he took her to a healer, questions would be asked—

questions neither of them could afford to answer. Plus, if she died, he wouldn't get more answers out of her. He would have to take her home.

Grimacing, he pulled her limp body into his arms and carefully stood. With difficulty, he opened her door and shuffled down the hallway. He paused in the dark, listening for any sign of life. If her crew caught him with her looking a mess, they would kill him on the spot and ask questions later. When no sound reached him, Hayjen swept across the deck and down to the dock. Drunken singing, crass jokes, and thundering waves filled the air around him. He pulled the hurt pirate closer in his arms and moved as speedily as he could. His heart practically beat out of his chest when he passed one of her crewmen. Luckily for him, they weren't paying any attention to him.

Wetness dripped down his arm and into the crook of his elbow. He gritted his teeth and picked up his speed. When the forge came into sight, relief filled him. His arms were practically shaking from carrying her so long. He didn't dare throw her over his shoulder because of her head wound. Hayjen cut across the yard and stormed into the dim kitchen. "Gwen!"

His sister and a rumpled looking Colm burst into the kitchen and halted, staring at the bloody woman in his arms.

Gwen's eyes snapped to him, an accusing light glowing in them. "What did you do?" she growled.

Shame filled him. He didn't cause all her injuries but he'd cut her. He hurt her.

His sister spun to the sink and began pulling towels and rags from her collection of healing supplies. "Put her on the table, Hayjen. Colm, could you heat up some water?"

Colm grunted and disappeared into the other room.

"Put her on the table."

"She has a wound on the back of her head, too."

Gwen glared over her shoulder at him before she turned back to her herbs and towel, angrily digging through them. "Lay her on her side then."

With care, he placed her on her side, making sure that she was covered by what was left of the robe.

"Get out of the way," Gwen growled, shoving him aside.

Hayjen stared, clenching and unclenching his hands. "What can I do to help?"

"You can get out," she said coldly.

"I want to help."

A hard laugh rumbled out of his sister as she placed a towel beneath Lilja's head. "By the looks of it, you've helped enough."

He glared at her, his emotions still high after the night he'd had. "I didn't do this."

"Sure, brother. You spoke of nothing but revenge earlier, and then you show up with a battered bloody woman in the middle of the night."

Colm bustled in with the hot water. "Where do you want this, sweetness?"

"In the bowl with the herbs."

He watched as she began to clean the large wound on the pirate's face. "She's going to need stitches. Hand me the whiskey, Hayjen."

Obediently, he grabbed the spirits and passed them to his sister. She poured the spirits over the sizeable cut. "That will kill whatever is in there. Colm, could you heat up my needle?" The large man nodded and disappeared out of the room again. "I am going to need your help holding her. It's going to hurt. She's passed out for now, but it won't be a pleasant experience for anyone."

Hayjen sat on the table and stared blankly at the pale woman on their table. He had caused this. What had he been thinking?

"Hell if I know."

His head snapped up.

"You were talking out loud," Gwen grumbled.

"Sorry."

"You should be."

Thoroughly chastised, he contented himself to hold the captain's hand while his sister readied the thread and needle. Gwen brushed aside Lilja's hair and froze, squinting at the straight pale lines on her neck.

"What in the hell?" she whispered, looking up at him with wide eyes. "What are those?"

"Gills."

"What?" she gasped, leaning closer to get a better look. "How?"

"I don't know."

"What is she?"

"A damn dirty Sirenidae," came a voice from behind them.

He and his sister both jerked and turned to see Joseph hovering in the doorway wearing a look of disgust. "Get that creature out of my home."

"She's hurt. She needs care."

The old man slashed his hand. "I won't have their kind in my home."

Gwen straightened. "I don't care what you think. I'm not throwing out an injured woman."

The old man's face reddened. "Now listen here, Gwen, you're like one of my own, but you don't understand what they can do to you. They're dangerous."

"Does she look dangerous to you?" Gwen flung a

hand out.

Joseph's lips thinned. "I don't like it."

"Well too bad. Go get some rest. You need it." His sister turned her back on Colm and his father. Colm ushered his father out of the room, then rushed back in with Gwen's needles.

Hayjen eyed the needle skeptically. "You sure you know what you are doing? You hate sewing."

His sister's scowl deepened. "I can sew a damn straight line. Butt out."

Colm hid a grin behind his wife's back that made Hayjen burst out laughing.

"Do you find this funny?"

"No," he gurgled. "It's just, could this night be odder?"

Her lips lifted into a slight grin. "I doubt it. Now quit messing around and hold her still."

He held her head and forced himself to watch as Gwen sewed the cut closed, one small stitch at a time. Lilja's eyes fluttered and one eye cracked open. "Gwen?"

"I know." She tied the thread and tugged. "Done."

Hayjen stared down at Lilja's one open eye. "It's okay, you're safe."

Quicker than he could have expected, she knocked him off the table. The air rushed out of him as he smashed into the floor and stared up at the woman crouched defensively on the table, her pupils blown wide. One hand clutched her head, the other held the bottle of spirits. Her odd eyes darted around the group of people.

"What do you want with me?"

Gwen held up her hands in surrender. "Nothing. You were hurt and we were helping you."

"With drugs and needles?" Lilja spat, shifting as her entire robe gaped open.

Colm's head snapped to the wall, studiously ignoring the body on display.

"I didn't give you any drugs. The herbs and spirits were to keep the wound from being infected. You managed to hit the front and back of your head. Also, your robe is open."

The pirate ran her hand to the back of her head and winced. "That hurts," she muttered, doing nothing about her nudity.

"I imagine so. If you'll get down from the table, I'll clean it and bind it for you, but you need to put the bottle down."

"I don't know you."

"I'm Gwen, that's my husband Colm, and the one on the floor gaping at you is Hayjen, my brother. I believe you know him already."

Her eyes latched onto the sight of him slipping the bottle from her fingers. "Indeed. I don't feel so good."

Hayjen kept his eyes on her face and launched from the floor, catching her before she fell off the table unconscious.

Gwen hurried to his side and closed Lilja's robe with a good knot. "We need to move her to a bedroom. Maybe we can tie her to the bed so she can't hurt herself."

"Tie her to the bed?" Colm questioned.

"Did you not just watch her almost hurt herself?"

"Yes, but don't you think it would scare her when she wakes up?"

"Good point, my love." She turned her gaze back on Hayjen. "I guess it's up to you to check on her all night. Did you see her eyes? She has a concussion."

"I thought so," he whispered as he stared into the captain's face. He lifted her body from the table and followed his sis through the house to his room. When he gave her a look, she shrugged.

"This is the only one available. It's not like you've been using it since you got here."

That was true.

He placed her on his bed and stepped back, allowing Gwen to work. Once his sister had arranged the bedding and the woman to her liking, she stepped to his side, still staring at Lilja.

"We have a lot to talk about in the morning."

Hayjen swallowed. "I know."

Gwen pierced him with a look when she glanced up. "I love you. Goodnight."

"Love you."

She placed a soft kiss on his cheek and tiptoed out of the room. He moved the chair from the corner next to the bed and groaned as he sat. What a night. Emotion after emotion rolled through him, wearing him out to the point where he just wanted to sleep so he could forget how stupid he'd been. Shame at what he had caused was still acute. Hayjen plucked the pirate's hand from the blanket and held it. "I'm sorry," he whispered. "I'm so sorry. I was wrong."

He was sure he'd pay for it.

Chapter Eleven

Lilja

Her head pounded.

What had she done last night?

Lilja cracked her eyes open and slammed them shut, the light causing pain to pierce behind her eyes. She lifted a hand to her head and whimpered when her whole body cried out. Why did everything bloody hurt?

"Shhhhh..." a male voice soothed. A large hand smoothed back her hair from her face. "You're okay."

She didn't feel okay. It was like she'd been thrown from a horse. Lilja wet her cracked lips and tried to speak, only managing a croak.

"One second."

A chair scraped back, causing the pain in her head to flare. Cool metal was pressed to her lips.

Reflexively, she opened her mouth and gulped down the cool water. She sighed as the water soothed her parched throat. "The light," Lilja murmured. Fabric rustled and then darkness descended. "Thank you."

She braved opening her eyes and peeked out of one at the room. It was simple. A sturdy side table, a trunk, and a large man in the corner. Her eyes widened at the sight of Hayjen. He looked haggard. His shirt was askew and stained, his hair rumpled, and dark circles under his eyes. "When's the last time you slept?" she blurted.

He barked out a chuckle. "Not a full night since Mer."

Mer.

Her breathing stuttered as she remembered the night before. Hayjen surprising her. Falling. Hayjen discovering her secret. The pain. Then darkness. His gaze never left her face as she remembered the night before. She had many questions, but she settled on, "Where am I?"

"My home."

That really shocked her. "Your home?"

"Do you remember anything?"

Lilja winced. "The last thing I remember is you scrambling away from me."

He frowned. "You hit your head."

"That would explain the pain."

His lips thinned further. "There was a lot of blood. I didn't know where to take you because of the..." he gestured to his neck. "So I brought you home. My sister knows a little healing."

Her hand went to her gills self-consciously. They had sealed completely. Hayjen's eyes rested there and then darted back to her eyes.

"She gave you stitches."

"Thank you for caring for me."

"Don't thank me. It's my fault you're hurt in the first place."

"It was an accident. You didn't mean to push me into the desk."

"I had a dagger at your neck."

True, but she didn't think he would have done it. "I spent enough time with you on that ship to know that you wouldn't hurt me, no matter what you said."

He shifted, agitation in the movement. "You're wrong. You don't know what I was thinking, Lilja." Hayjen's eyes squeezed shut. "I wanted to hurt you."

Sympathy filled her. "Grief tends to change us."

"That doesn't excuse my actions."

"No," she sighed, "but it explains them. Lucky for you, grief and I have been close companions in the past. So I am familiar with how it works."

Hayjen lifted his eyes, shame coating him like a cloak. "I am so sorry."

"I know, and I forgive you."

Shock filled his face. "I don't deserve it."

"Most of us don't." Lilja carefully pushed up from the bed, ignoring the pain. "That's why forgiveness is so precious. It's a gift."

Silence filled the room as he took that in. He nodded to himself and gestured to the chair. "May I sit?"

"It's your house."

He smiled at that, managing a chuckle as he sat. They gazed at each other in silence for a few minutes before he spoke up. "So where does that leave us?"

"Us?" she questioned.

"Are you going to hurt my family?"

She frowned at him, making her headache even worse. "Why would I do that?"

"We know your secret."

That was a problem. "Can I trust you? Can your family take my secret to the grave? It's not just my life that depends on it."

"We will keep silent."

"Then we don't have a problem."

He leaned toward her and stared harder.

Lilja stared back. "Something interesting?"

"Where did they go?" he asked curiously.

She gestured to her neck. "They seal after a couple hours. They're only visible after I have been in the ocean."

"Huh," he grunted. "And Mer?"

"She won't get her gills until she hits puberty."

Another grunt.

"Use your words." she teased.

"I had a lot of time to think last night. If I hadn't seen your g-gills," he stuttered over the word, "I wouldn't have believed you. It's hard to come to terms with the fact that not everything is as it seems in the world."

"Some truths are a burden to bear."

"Indeed." Hayjen lifted his scarred wrists. "Sometimes we wear them, too."

"You're not alone," she whispered, staring over his head. "The Scythians will pay for what they've done."

"That sounds personal."

"It is personal."

"Care to share?"

Her eyes dropped to his steady gaze. He opened his arms with a wry smile. "You saved and jailed me. I've threatened and fought with you. You're one of the few that know I was captured by the Scythians, and I'm one of the few that know you're a Sirenidae. We're practically family."

She chuckled at his warped logic. "Oddly, that makes sense."

"I saw how you looked at the Scythians on the

slaver ship. More than justice was in your eyes. You were seeking vengeance."

Her laughter died as she sobered. "They took something very precious from me." Lilja stared into his blue eyes and found herself wanting to tell him her story, to commiserate. "Many years ago, the Sirenidae decided to recede from society. They could see what Scythia was becoming. They could see the perversion in their ideals, so they disappeared into the sea and away from the kingdoms. Every hundred years or so the decision would be revisited and voted on again. It was safer for our people to stay below, but there was one Sirenidae that thought it was wrong to leave the kingdoms ignorant of Scythia's experiments. She wanted to help *all* people, not just her own. She held ideals that maybe Scythia had changed over the years—that maybe they could change with the proper perspective."

"You."

She met his eyes. "Me." Lilja dropped her eyes to her lap. "Sirenidae live a long time and are wise, but even so, they're not perfect. I was expected to fall in line when my opinion was not the consensus, but I couldn't let go. I had the power to help, so it was my duty to do so. One thing led to another and I was given a choice. Stay and follow the rules, or leave and never return. So I left." She smiled bitterly. "I was so hopeful when I entered Scythia. I was going to change the world, make a difference. By all appearances, Scythia seemed to be thriving and peaceful. It was nothing like I was raised to believe. I was welcomed warmly and lulled into a false sense of security. The warlord was utterly charming—the picture of beauty and hospitality."

She lifted the cup and took a drink, hoping it would fortify her to tell the rest of her story. Lilja placed the cup in her lap and met Hayjen's concerned eyes. "I never saw it coming. I became very tired during dinner and retired early to my room. The next moment, I was strapped to an odd table in a room made of material I'd never seen before. Healers came and went, poking me with sharp needles and making me drink different concoctions. I asked many questions but no one would answer me.

"One day the warlord visited me. He looked the same as ever and yet there was this glint in his eyes that made the hair on my arms stand up." Lilja shivered, but continued. "I asked why he had imprisoned me. Do you know what his answer was?"

Hayjen shook his head no.

"That animals deserved to be chained."

Hayjen cursed.

"That was my reaction, too. He laughed at me and

said that despite my disgusting heritage, I would change the world just like I wanted to. A very large warrior entered at that point and stood in the corner, watching the spectacle." She paused to gather her thoughts, ignoring the sick feeling churning in her gut. "After the Nagalian purge, many Scythians were wiped out in the aftermath of the war. Because of their ideals, they kept experimenting with their people. Striving for perfection."

"That's what caused the Nagalian purge in the first place," said Hayjen. "They believed the Nagali people were an abomination."

"Indeed. But something happened that they didn't anticipate. Their women couldn't bear children. The warlord explained all of this to me and said that this was where I came in. To breed more little warriors, they needed fertile women."

Horror morphed Hayjen's face as he connected the dots. "That's why there were so many women on the slaver ship."

"Yes," she gritted out. "Since women were scarce, only his most faithful warriors received brood mares." Lilja waved her hand as tears pricked her eyes. "I will spare you the details, but I unwillingly became pregnant."

A stifling silence filled the room. "Oh Lil, I'm so sorry." A pause. "The baby?"

"I lost her." Hot tears filled her eyes. "I had enough one day and I fought back. It was an accident. I pushed too hard and he pushed back."

The bed dipped and large arms wrapped around her. "Those bastards."

A tear slipped down her face. "But I was right. Not all of the Scythians were bad. There was one who was willing to sacrifice everything to help me escape."

"Blair," Hayjen breathed onto the top of her head.

"He was the bunkmate of the warrior I was given to, so we lived together. He protected me and took care of me while I was pregnant."

"I just—there aren't words."

She wiped her face. "No, there aren't. Nothing can describe the helplessness of being taken over and over again without a choice. It pales to the pain you feel when you lose a child. You lose part of yourself that won't ever heal." They sat there in silence holding each other as her tears dried. Lilja looked up into Hayjen's pained face. "I understand what you're feeling right now. The anger will turn into something ugly unless you channel it into something positive."

"Like you have?"

"Like I have. I protect others from my fate." Lilja pulled away her head, which was pounding harder after her crying. "That's why I need to return to my ship. We accomplish important work."

"I want to help."

Lilja froze and turned to him. "What?"

"I want to help. What can I do?"

She placed a hand on top of his. "Live a happy life with your family."

"Gwen's married."

Her lips pursed. "I know."

He gave her an odd look. "How?"

She shrugged.

Hayjen shook his head. "Never mind. It doesn't matter. I have no place here."

"What are you talking about?" She stabbed a finger at the door. "You have a family right outside that door."

"My whole life has been about raising and taking care of Gwen, but now she has someone else to take care of her."

"That doesn't mean she doesn't need you."

"No, but she's a woman now. She has her own life and now I can choose my own."

"What are you saying?"

"I want to leave with you on the Sirenidae."

Lilja gaped at him. "A day ago you wanted to kill me, and now you want to join my crew?"

"A lot has changed in that time. I want to make a difference, and I don't want anyone to suffer as I did.

It seems like joining your crew is the best option."

She blinked. "That's a big decision."

"It is."

"It's a hard life."

"My life has always been hard."

Lilja changed her tactic. "Have you told Gwen?"

"No."

"Speak with your family before you make any hasty decisions." She stood and moved to leave.

"Where are you going?" Hayjen asked, standing from the bed.

"To my ship."

"You're hurt."

"I'm fine. My head hardly hurts."

His eyes narrowed.

Lilja unwrapped her hand and held it to the big man. "I heal quickly." The cut on her hand was sealed and a shiny pink color.

"Seriously?" he growled.

"What?"

"You heal at an extraordinary rate, too?"

"Sirenidae."

"I'll escort you back to the ship."

She held her hand up. "I would prefer to go back by myself. Thank you for caring for me." Lilja opened the door and paused, looking over her shoulder. "We leave port tomorrow at dawn."

With that parting remark, she slipped out of the room and down a hallway to the kitchen. A petite brunette woman with hazel eyes smiled at her from the table.

"How's your head?"

"Fine, thanks to you I'm told," Lilja replied with a smile.

The brunette stood and offered her hand. "I'm Gwen."

"Lilja. I hate to be ungrateful, and I wish I could stay, but I must return to my ship. Thank you for your care, and for sharing your home with me."

Gwen moved to the door and opened it. "My pleasure. Safe travels."

Lilja surprised the woman by hugging her before she left the home. Outside, she set a brisk pace toward the fishing district. Blair was probably ripping apart the dock searching for her. She grimaced. He would not be happy.

Chapter Twelve

Lilja

She sucked in the salty air as she meandered down the dock to the Sirenidae. She couldn't believe how much had changed in the last day. Exhausted as she was, happiness bubbled beneath the surface. Lilja had fixed things with Hayjen. He was no longer out for revenge, or hating her for a crime she didn't commit. That was a success in her book.

A shout went up when she arrived at the Sirenidae. She inhaled a deep breath. It was time for the interrogation. Lilja smiled broadly as she boarded, her crew huddling around her.

"You okay, Captain?" Johnathan asked, gesturing to her head.

"I just took a nasty fall."

"It was some fall. It took hours to get the blood

out of your carpets."

Lilja forced a smile to her face and held Blair's gaze. "Yes, well, you know head wounds bleed a lot." She gestured to herself. "As you can see, I am in perfect health. Now, prepare the ship. We leave at dawn." With her dismissal, her crew dispersed, leaving Blair glaring at her.

"Would you like a word, First Mate?" she asked while moving to her study.

"Indeed I would, Captain," he growled.

Lilja noted the absence of her favorite rug as she entered her study. She turned and sat in the window seat. "I'm sorry."

Blair crossed his arms, eyeing her. "Are you okay?"

"I am."

"That was a lot of blood, Lil."

"I was taken care of."

"By whom?"

"A friend," she hedged.

He sighed, running a hand through his hair. "I was so worried. I had men sent out discreetly to find you. You didn't leave a note."

"Well, I was kind of unconscious."

Blair scowled at the sarcasm in her voice. "It's not funny."

She held her thumb and pointer finger together. "It is a little bit."

"I was worried."

Lilja dropped her teasing. "I know. I didn't mean to worry you, but I'm okay. I had an accident."

"How did you get to a healer?"

"Hayjen took me."

Blair's eyes widened. "Hayjen? How did Hayjen get on the bloody ship?" His face darkened. "Did he do this to you? Are you protecting him, Lil? So help me if—"

"He didn't crack my head open. We did fight," she explained, "but we're on good terms now."

"How?"

"He knows."

He stiffened. "Please don't tell me you were stupid enough to tell him."

"Hey now," she cautioned. "I am not stupid. It was the Lure."

"The Lure?"

"Yeah—what you experienced last night?"

He blanched.

"He caught me off guard. We fought, he saw my gills, and I passed out. He took me to his sister. They took very good care of me and promised to stay silent about my heritage."

"And you trust them?"

"I do."

Blair kept silent, thinking things over before blowing out a breath. "Okay."

"Okay?"

He flashed her a faint smile. "Okay." He stared at the floor for a beat before meeting her eyes. "I need to speak to you about something."

Her stomach dropped at the tone of his voice. "What?"

"Last night I made a decision."

"A serious one?"

"Indeed." He blew out a breath and met her gaze squarely. "I'm going back."

"No," she breathed, staring at him in horror. "No, you can't."

"I can and I will."

"No, I won't allow you to." Lilja jumped to her feet. "I will never let you go back to that hellhole."

"I have to."

"Why?" she cried.

"We need to know what's going on beyond the wall. We need someone on the inside."

"They'll kill you on sight."

"They think I'm dead. They don't know I escaped with you."

"You're just one person."

"I can help the slaves there."

Lilja's eyes filled with tears. His decision was final. She saw it in the way he stood. "You're leaving me?" she asked, her voice cracking.

Blair's stern face melted into sorrow. He pulled

her from the window seat and wrapped his arms around her. "You don't need me."

The tears burst free. "I'll always need you," she sobbed into his shirt. "How can you leave me? Is it because of what the Lure did to you last night?"

He pulled her wet face from his shirt. "The Lure is the least of our problems."

His face blurred. "Then why now?"

Gentle fingers wiped the tears from her face and serious, deep brown eyes searched her eyes for something. "I've felt this way for a long time. The only reason I didn't leave sooner is because I wasn't ready to part with you, and I knew you needed me. You don't need me anymore, Lil. You haven't for a long time."

"What are you talking about? You're my first mate and my best friend."

"Can you survive without me?"

"Yes."

"Can you run this ship on your own?"

"Yes," she stuttered out.

"You want me here, but you don't need me. Others need me, Lil."

Her heart squeezed painfully. "I don't want you to go. I'll never see you again."

His hand clasped her face. "I am going to ask you a question and I want a serious answer."

"Okay," she hiccupped.

"Do you want me?"

"Of course I want you."

"No," he tipped her chin up with his thumbs and leaned closer. "Do you want me?"

Understanding dawned, and blue eyes flashed through her mind. "No." It was one of the hardest things she had ever had to say.

He smiled. "It's okay."

"Do you?" she left the question hanging in the air.

"No, but I love you."

"I love you, too." A tear dripped down her cheek.

Blair kissed the tear away. "We're comfortable with each other and that's okay. But I saw how you looked at Hayjen. I've been waiting for the time you would finally show interest in someone. We have been to hell and back, but we need to move forward. That's the only way to live a healthy life."

"If you go, I'll never see you again."

"This is not goodbye. I am widening your scope of spies. We can take Scythia down, but only if we have someone on the inside."

Lilja placed her ear against his heart and hugged him tightly as the last of her tears dried. "Can you go back to that life?"

"I have to." Blair's arms tightened around her.

She leaned back and held onto his forearms. "Can you hold onto yourself?"

"I'll have to."

"Blair," she said softly, "the life of a spy is painful."

"If my suffering can save hundreds and thousands of others, it will be worth it."

"You're a good person." She stepped out of his arms and scrubbed at her face. Her best friend was leaving her, but she understood why. "How long until you leave?"

He smiled sadly. "Tomorrow morning."

A small sound of pain escaped her. "So soon?" she croaked, trying to keep it together.

Tears flooded her dearest friend's face. "The Mort Wall is close." He pulled her back into a fierce hug. Wet drops plopped onto the top of her face, causing her tears to burst free. "Leaving you will be the hardest thing I've ever done."

"If I could go with you I would."

"I know."

They held each other and cried until no more tears were left. Lilja didn't want their last day spent together to be drowned in sorrow. She tilted her head back and smiled. "How about a swim?" He loved swimming.

Blair grinned. "That's a perfect idea."

"First one inked by an octopus has to buy drinks."

"You're on."

Chapter Thirteen

Hayjen

The last day on the land was the best day he had since he arrived home. He spent the morning helping Colm in the forge, and then helped Gwen with household chores in the afternoon. The evening passed with a divine stew and hearty bread that his sister had perfected. Hayjen sat near the hearth drinking his brew before bed when Gwen sat next to him and laid a hand over his.

"When do you leave?"

Startled, his eyes flew to his sister's. "What?"

"You're stir-crazy here. I can see it, and I heard part of your conversation this morning."

He clasped her hand. "Would you be angry if I did?"

"No, but I'll be sad. I finally have you back."

"I wouldn't be gone forever. I will be home every couple of months."

Gwen studied him in her keen way. "You don't have to explain yourself to me. This is your life. You've been living for me since papa and mum died. It's okay to make choices for you. I'm well cared for."

She'd grown up. Hayjen could hardly believe it. It felt like just yesterday his mum was placing Gwen in his chubby little arms. Soon there would be a new little one. "I'll be here for the babe as much as I can."

She smiled and touched her belly. "It's hard to believe I created life."

"It's wondrous."

"It is." She lifted her eyes. "Will you be in danger?"

Hayjen couldn't lie to her. "Yes."

Her jaw tightened and she looked away. "Can you tell me any specifics?"

"I am going to protect others from what happened to me."

"As a pirate," she stated carefully.

"Yes."

Gwen nodded and met his gaze. "I support you in this completely, but after the baby is born, we need to be careful."

His actions from here on out would put his family in danger. "We'll work something out."

"Even if it means no contact except through

letters?"

He swallowed. "If that's what it takes to protect you and your family."

"I don't think it will come to that, but we need to think about the consequences." Tears filled Gwen's eyes. "I want you to be happy."

Hayjen stood and wrapped his arms around her. "You've made me a happy uncle."

He stuffed his last shirt into his sack and swung it over his shoulder. Hayjen scanned the little room, smiling at the touches of his sister here and there. He closed the door behind him and moved through the quiet house to the kitchen. Through the window, he could see Gwen standing in the tall grass, haloed by the sun. He smiled and slipped out of the kitchen to her side.

"All ready to go?" she whispered.

"I am."

Gwen turned to him, a wobbly smile on her face. "I always wanted to be a pirate, and now I'm related to one. So that makes me one by extension. Pirate Gwen Blackwell has a nice ring to it."

Hayjen sniggered and held open his arms. "Come here." His sister rushed into his arms and held him so tightly he swore his ribs creaked.

"I love you," she murmured into his vest.

"I love you too, baby girl."

"When shall I expect you?"

"In the next couple months."

"You'll be back before the baby?"

"I wouldn't miss it for the world." He lifted his head as Colm wandered in their direction and stood behind Gwen. Hayjen let go of his sister and clasped hands with the younger man. Colm surprised him and jerked him into a hug with a lot of back-slapping.

"Safe travels."

He grinned at his brother-in-law. "Will do." Hayjen grabbed his sister for a last hug and pecked her on the cheek. "I'll be back soon."

"I'll hunt you down if you aren't," she sniffed, huddling into her husband's side.

That brought a smile to his face. "I don't doubt it."

Hayjen waved and strode in the direction of the fishing market. It amazed him how quiet and peaceful everything was. Nervous energy filled him when he reached the bustling docks. How would the Sirenidae crew react to him?

A dark, familiar person moved in his direction, carrying a rucksack like his. "Blair?" His head snapped in Hayjen's direction and his eyes sharpened. The first mate halted in front of him.

"Hayjen."

"Isn't the Sirenidae leaving?"

"Yes."

"You're going in the wrong direction," Hayjen pointed out slowly.

"I have a new assignment. I'm on leave."

"Enjoy your leave." He moved around the dark man.

"Hayjen."

He paused and met Blair's serious eyes. "Take care of her."

Understanding passed between the two men. "I will."

"She needs someone like you."

He blinked. "I'm not sure what you mean."

Blair smirked. "Don't lie to yourself."

"Wise words."

"They're Lil's."

"Figures."

Both of them grinned at each other. "Best of luck on your new journey." Hayjen held out his hand.

Blair clasped it. "Same to you."

Hayjen watched him disappear into the crowd before turning and lifting his eyes to the Sirenidae. His future was right in front of him if he was brave enough to take it. A silver-haired beauty leaned over the railing, shock racing across her face. He waved and she lifted a hand in greeting, a smile blossoming on her face. His breath rushed out of him at the sight of her smile. He was right. His future was staring at him with magenta-colored eyes.

Epilogue

Hayjen

He stared at the shrinking bay, the large ships appearing like child's toys bobbing in the wave. There was no going back now. He peeked out of the corner of his eye at Lilja. "So what's our next step?"

"We wait."

His eye brows lowered. "We wait?"

Lilja smiled. "Yes, we wait."

"And what are we waiting for?"

"Change."

Change. It was sometimes slow and elusive. "And until then?" Hayjen asked.

Her smiled became fierce. "We sabotage and thwart Scythia in every way we can."

His smile mirrored hers, all vengeance and mischief. "Togther."

"Together," Lilja echoed.

The End

Thank you for reading Siren's Lure! If you fell in love with Lilja and Hayjen, continue the Aermian Feuds Series in book one, Rebel's Blade. Grab your free sample here!
https://www.frostkay.net/

About the Author

Frost Kay is a certified bookdragon with an excessive TBR, and a shoe obsession. Her goals in life include: Eating a five-pound bag of skittles in one sitting, creating worlds that sweep you away and leave you dazed, and preventing the cat from laying on top of her laptop.

She has an evil side she only let's out on special occasions, like at the end of a book...cliff hangers...the girl seriously loves them. If you hate bewitching stories, epic adventures, untold secrets, dark promises, thrilling action, swoon worthy anti-hero's, and slow burning romance her books aren't for you. If you do, well, you're in good company!

Read More from Frost Kay
www.frostkay.net

95956087R00109

Made in the USA
Columbia, SC
18 May 2018